Mighty Fine

Linda Voelker

TJT Designs and Publications

TJT Designs and Publications
12138 Central Ave Suite 869
Mitchellville, MD 20721

Copyright © 2015 by TJT Designs and Publications

All rights reserved, including the right to reproduce this book or portions thereof in any form whatsoever. Distributed by TJT Designs and Publications. For information address Tiffany Thomas/ TJT Designs and Publications, 12138 Central Ave Suite 869, Mitchellville, MD 20721

First TJT Designs and Publications paperback edition June 2013

For information about special discounts for bulk purchases, please contact TJT Designs and Publications at (866)-379-5983, Fax (866)-929-5113 or www.tjtdesigns.com/contact.

TJT Designs and Publications can bring authors to your live event. For more information contact TJT Designs and Publications at (866)-379-5983, Fax (866)-929-5113 or www.tjtdesigns.com/contact.

Cover Designed by Steven Scott

Manufactured in the United States of America

10 9 8 7 6 5 4 3 2

ISBN print   978-1-942663-95-9
     ebook   978-1-942663-96-6

Library of Congress Control Number:

Acknowledgments

    This is dedicated to Marilyn Moore. My mother, my sideick, my best friend. I love you so. And to my sons, Justin and Jeremy, who have grown in the blink of my eye from my preciious babes to two men that never cease to make me proud. I know what it is to be blessed by all of you and I'm humbled by it.

1

Rita was still laughing over something Tina had said as Jack and Dave joined them It had become a weekend ritual to cheer their husbands on during the softball season, and always a fun way to be together. Tonight was even more fun. The guys won.

Rita gave her husband, who was hot and sweaty, a hug in spite of it. "Good game, babe."

Jack looked rather smug, tossing her his glove as he gloated, "Yeah, did you see that double play? For an old man, pushin' forty, I can still work that field."

Tina nodded toward the horribly stained pants he wore, her eyes twinkling. "And now poor Rita gets to work on that crud – which will undoubtedly corrode the washing machine."

"Shhhhhhh," Rita half teased. "It's been making a clunking sound lately. I think it's on its last legs."

"Oh," Dave deadpanned, removing his baseball cap to scratch his head. "You mean you use yours? Tina thinks it's a decoration in the laundry room. I'm always reminding her how important it is to actually do the laundry and not let it pile up."

Tina shot him the stink eye. "Keep it up, Dave, and you'll be reminding me of other things, too."

He laughed and hugged her to his side. "You know I'm teasing, Teen. Hey..." He looked at Jack who was knocking

Mighty Fine

the mud from his shoes. "Want to stop at Vito's for pizza to celebrate, old man?"

Rita bit her lip, knowing they couldn't. Money was always too tight.

"No, I had a bet with that pretty lady over there, holding my mitt," he countered with a smile. "I trust she won't need reminding it's time to pay up," he winked, his implication clear.

Rita felt her face heat as they laughed, Tina's nudge strong enough to make her teeter. "You go, girl."

"Well, I won the bet," Rita smiled, swatting Jack with the glove.

"Till you collect," Dave laughed, as Tina yanked him toward the car, singing out, "See you guys. Have fun!"

Rita sighed when they were alone. It was pretty bad when you couldn't afford to go out with your friends for a cheap night out. "Money stinks."

Jack smiled, leaning on the car to pull her close, his eyes meeting hers. "We'll be fine, Hon. It's just a little rut in the road. Better days are coming, isn't that your mantra?"

Snuggling close to nuzzle his neck she whispered, "I love you, Jack."

"You better, woman. I'd hate to be in this alone." She felt his hand clap off her bottom before he set her back from him. "Let's get home so we can work on that bet thing."

She smiled, feeling the need to remind him, "We didn't really make a bet."

"Good, the odds are in my favor then," he deadpanned.

Linda Voelker

Rita laughed, getting in the car for the short drive home.

There was something to be said for living in Ohio, not that she'd ever lived anywhere else. But soon it would be fall, the leaves were already starting to change. She even loved winter. The first snowfall, anyway. Jack turned up the radio to sing along with Steve Perry, bringing her focus back to him. His wavy dark hair was a tad too long, but on him, it looked good. Everything about him looked good to Rita. He had the most amazing sky blue eyes, and a smile that could charm one and all. He was still the only man that could make her heart trip just seeing him, and that was saying something after eight years of marriage. While it was true that they were living from paycheck to paycheck most times, they were rich in all the ways that mattered.

She still thanked God for bringing them together. By the time they'd met she'd all but given up on finding a man to love. She had just turned thirty and all of her friends had married nearly a decade earlier. In fact, she met him a few days before the last in her circle of friends were wed.

She'd been heading to the bridal shop to pick up her bridesmaid's dress when her car just died. About a zillion cars seemed to fly by before Jack stopped. Rita had nervously inched her window down a crack, sure he was some crazed maniac out to get her as he had been the only one to stop, but he turned out to be a Godsend. He had her pop the hood and tinkered with something, getting it to start. Then, because he wanted to make sure it didn't choke out on her again, he followed her to the mall, waiting while she ran in to pick up the dress she was to wear that

Mighty Fine

weekend for Laci's wedding. Jack had insisted on buying her lunch before following her home. Who would have thought one could fall in love at the food court in the mall? But they did.

Jack pulled into the driveway and opened his door. He looked at her and said, "Bet I get inside quicker than you." He leaned to cup her head to kiss her. "As soon as you catch up, we both will," he added in a meaningful, lusty way.

She barely had time to recover from his kiss before he was sprinting to the door, only to disappear inside. She was still grinning as she joined him.

And for the record, he was right. They both knew they'd won in love a little while later, entwined in the tangled sheets.

A few days later Rita was finishing the dinner dishes as Jack changed the brakes on the car. Inspection was due, and as it was, they'd hold their breath till it passed.

"Hey, Rita!"

She dried her hands and went to the door, smiling. "Yeah?"

He was still halfway under the car as he reminded her, "Don't forget tonight is the drawing for that lottery ticket."

"Oh, you're right. I better find it then."

He chuckled, muttering, "Yeah, good luck with that."

She went in search, knowing that she would need luck to find it. She had a reputation for misplacing things, like her keys and her reading glasses. There were even a few times she forgot where she parked the car when she was out.

Moving to their desk in the corner of the dining room, she leafed through the clutter, discouraged by the bills that were due.

Linda Voelker

How could two people that worked so hard, owe so much?

Poor Jack worked overtime at the cable company as often as he could to make ends meet. Rita was always covering at the diner for call offs, but with the economy what it was, tips weren't what they once were. Winning the lottery would sure be nice. Not that she thought they would. But still...

"Ah...there you are," she smiled, plucking it out of the stack. She turned on the TV just as the little balls were jumping in the bin waiting to make someone's dreams come true. Kissing the ticket, she whispered, "Why not ours?"

"Six..." She glanced at the ticket and tapped the six, "Good ball."

"Twenty seven..." She grinned, having that one too.

"Thirteen..." She felt a tingle dance down her spine.

"Forty..." Her hand shook a bit as she acknowledged it was there as well.

"And the last number is--Two."

Jack came in a moment later, finding Rita standing ramrod straight in front of the TV. She was pale and looked frozen in place.

"Rita? Honey?" He immediately worried when she didn't even glance his way. He moved to her and cupped her chin, his eyes showing his concern. "Baby, what's wrong? Are you okay?"

"L-Lottery..."

He smiled in relief. "You missed it?"

"W-We won," she managed before she started to tremble.

Jack chuckled, kissing her forehead. "We did, huh? What

Mighty Fine

was it? Ten, twenty bucks?" In truth, even that would be cause to celebrate.

"Th-Thirty million," she rasped, her eyes searching his as she squeaked, "We won!"

He took the ticket she thrust his way and frowned, sure she was mistaken. "Rita...honey..."

"We did...we did...Jack...we did!"

He moved to the rebuilt computer and went to the lottery site, deciding to placate her and also prove her wrong. By the time he'd checked the ticket twice, he was numb.

"Rita...did you...I mean...how..." Logically, he knew she couldn't have made this ticket, but just as logically, he knew they couldn't have won. Could they?

Rita was blinking back tears as she crowed, "See?!!"

Jack looked at the ticket once more, checking with determination to find an error. When he couldn't, he stood and gathered her close to swing her in circles. "We WON! Baby—we hit the lottery!"

As he twirled her in circles he didn't know whether to laugh or cry, but Rita latched onto the latter, sobbing as she clung to him. Their money worries would be over. They could go out for pizza three times a day if they wanted! They could pay off all their bills and still have money left over!

Feeling as if they were in a dream, they spent the rest of the night talking over what the win would mean for them.

"We can travel, sweetheart. You always wanted to go to Hawaii. Now we can go!" Jack was stroking her hip as she sat curled up on his lap, her heart still going a mile a minute.

"We can pay off everything, Jack. We won't have any more window envelopes in the mail!"

He grinned and kissed her temple, tugging her blonde hair playfully. "We can do anything we want to, baby." He shifted on the couch, nearly toppling her from her perch. "We can go to the Superbowl!"

She laughed at his genuine excitement over that prospect. "Yes...and Jack, we can get a new roof and insulation! Our heating bills will go down," she grinned, remembering last winter when the gas bill alone was like the national debt.

"We can get a new house to put under that roof, woman. Think big!"

"But I love our house," she frowned. It was filled with memories and she couldn't imagine leaving.

"You'll love our new one too," he grinned.

"Think about work, Jack! No more overtime for you... won't that be something?"

"Baby, we won't have to work anymore. No more greasy spoon or rude customers. We can live well the rest of our lives without a hitch."

She was lost for a moment in that thought, then sat straight to cup his face in her hands. "Jack...promise me something."

"What's that, Hon?"

Her green eyes locked with his. "Promise me we won't let the money change us."

He snorted, finding the thought preposterous. "No way, no

Mighty Fine

how, sweetheart. Even knowing how lucky we are tonight, the day we met will always be the luckiest day of my life."

Her eyes puddled up with emotional tears as she kissed him, for he'd just relieved all her fears. Snuggling closer to him she whispered, "Okay, you can turn in the ticket."

Jack's bark of laughter soon filled the house, her giggles going along for the ride.

2

The next few days after the win were crazy. They retained a lawyer who told them not to do anything at all, other than sign the back of the ticket so nobody else could cash it in if it were lost or stolen.

"But, wouldn't it be better to just turn it in?" Rita felt the pressure of keeping it weighing heavy. Her track record for losing things was legendary.

Glenn, a middle aged attorney that they'd found in the phone book shook his head. "Not just yet. It's now time for you to get your thoughts straight on what you want to do. You need to decide if you're going to take a lump sum or get your money in payments. Tax issues come into play. And you want to make the money work for you, as well. You need to find a financial adviser. Someone that has a good reputation in their field." He opened a drawer and brought out a card file, flipping through as he searched for ones he might suggest. "Here are a few I know," he said, jotting the names and numbers down to slide across the desk.

Rita was a nervous wreck, the excitement of last night, shifting into something akin to fear. "Jack, I don't think we should keep that ticket in the house. What if we lose it? What if the house catches fire? What if we get robbed?"

Mighty Fine

Jack bit back a smile and gave her hand a squeeze. "You worry too much."

Glenn smiled softly as well. "Do you have a safety deposit box at the bank?"

"No, we don't," Jack replied, "I'll look into that when we leave."

"Another thing," Glenn warned. "I wouldn't tell anyone you won. Not even family, if you're unsure they can keep it to themselves. Once word gets out, you'll find yourself bombarded by the media. You won't be able to leave your house to grab the paper from your porch when word's out."

Rita bit her lip. "We don't even get the paper anymore. We just get the Sunday one for the coupons. Sometimes." She looked at Glenn. "We cut corners where we could."

Jack kissed the hand he held. "We don't have to cut corners anymore, babe."

Glenn hated to interrupt, but added, "Check broker records at the Financial Industry Regulatory Authority. Don't just take those numbers and think that they're stellar. Things change and I haven't checked them in about a month."

Rita frowned, shifting on the chair. "They can go bad that fast?"

"Financial matters fluctuate quickly. Just be diligent. Don't take anyone's word for things. Check them out yourself. You're entering a new world now."

Jack wished he hadn't brought Rita because she would make herself sick if she kept dwelling on things. "Well, Glenn, we appreciate your help." He stood and shook his hand, smiling. "We'll go the bank and I'll check those firms you gave us."

"Just remember," Glenn smiled, "This isn't a race. You have a few months to decide your next steps."

Rita found herself shaking his hand too, tons of questions still swirling in her head. "Should we put the money in CD's? Or maybe a 401K?" Looking at Jack she smiled. "We can finally open a savings account!"

Jack laughed and hugged her to his side. "We'll be seeing you, Glenn. Thanks again."

Glenn chuckled after they left, for he could hear Rita saying, "What's wrong with CD's? And I always thought those 401k's were a good thing."

The woman had no clue what becoming a millionaire meant for them. He went back to his desk, hoping it didn't change them too much. They seemed like a great couple.

An hour later they left the bank and Jack had to laugh. "Ree...you need to relax. You look like we just robbed the bank, for Pete's sake."

Actually, she felt like she had. "Why is this so hard? And Martha must think I'm so rude, Jack! I was afraid to even look, look at her for fear she'd see we'd won on my face. I was actually terrified she'd ask what was new and I'd blurt it out!"

"It's just until we get our ducks in a row, babe." Jack opened her car door and when she got in, he went around to get in behind

Mighty Fine

the wheel. "It's all going to be fine, Ree. Just don't worry so much, okay?"

"We're in over our heads," she whispered, looking like she wanted to cry.

Jack smiled at her tenderly. "Do you trust me?"

"Of course I do."

"Then just let me worry about the money, okay? I'll work on finding the right financial adviser and you just start thinking about a new house or where we'll travel to first."

Her heart tripped at the very thought and she struggled to find a smile. "You must think I'm so silly, Jack, I don't know why I'm scared."

He pulled her close and held her, "It's a big change, that's all. Actually, I'm a bit unnerved too."

She pulled back to search his face, "Really?"

Jack gave a nod, then kissed her softly, "But this is our happily ever after, Ree. Everything is going to be wonderful. You'll see."

Rita smiled, hugging him tight before she gasped. "Oh, I'm going to be late for work!"

He laughed, starting the car. "You don't have to go back, you know. We won the lottery."

"No," she frowned, "I promised Luella I'd cover for her. Her son's sick."

Only Rita, he thought, loving her all the more, "Okay, babe. But once we get things settled, you're hanging up your apron."

She smiled, having no problem with that idea at all.

Linda Voelker

The diner was moderately filled with the usual patrons, all of them calling out a greeting to Rita as she entered. Jimmy, the owner, frowned at her, as she went back to clock in.

"You're late, Rita."

"Sorry, Jimmy. We got caught up at the bank." She grabbed her order pad and tucked her pen in her pocket, smiling up at him. "Did I ever thank you for hiring me?"

Jim looked at her, wondering where that came from, "You're late. I'm not firing you."

She giggled and gave his back a pat, "I know. I just appreciated working here more than I can say."

Rita went out to work the counter as Jimmy snorted and shook his head smiling. Rita was his favorite, but she sure came out with some odd things.

Jack, meanwhile, printed his bank statement on the computer, checking to make sure they'd deposited his last pay. Just the thought of it being his last, rather than his most recent, made him smile. He had planned on going in tomorrow and just walking back to Harry and saying he quit, but why waste the gas?

Harry Jones was a scrawny guy that let his position go to his head. He was great at belittling the crew members in front of others, knowing they needed their jobs so they'd take it. Jack would be thrilled to see the last of him.

He punched in the telephone number he knew by heart, asking for Harry before being put on hold. He imagined Harry

Mighty Fine

scowling, thinking he was calling off, but he rarely did that. Neither did Rita, for that matter. She worked her own shifts and filled in for others all the time. Jack was happier that his wife could quit than he was for himself.

"Yeah, Brown, what is it?"

Jack smiled, "How ya doin' Harry?"

"I'm busy. Did you need something?"

"Yes," Jack grinned, glad Harry was so out of patience. It sure made it easier. "Just letting you know I won't be back in."

Harry sighed, "Sick day or vacation day?"

"Guess you would consider it a vacation day, as are all the ones to follow. I'll be in to get my things sometime next week."

Jack listened to the silence that hung between them for a few seconds, before Harry barked, "You quit?! You telling me you quit, Brown?"

"Yep." Jack wondered if his grin could grow any wider as he heard Harry sputter.

"Tell the crew I said goodbye, buddy. Take care now."

And as Harry tried to fathom it all, Jack ended the call and chuckled. It felt even better than he'd imagined.

He then pulled out the paper from the lawyer and started researching names they'd be given.

Rita was torn as she waited for Jack to pick her up at midnight. It was bittersweet to think she wouldn't be back to the diner. She hadn't said anything to Jimmy or to the other girls, but she

Linda Voelker

knew she was officially done. She even hugged Stanley, the most miserable of her customers, who came in to complain about each and every thing she served. She knew he was just lonely after his wife passed away.

She glanced at the clock over the counter and frowned, wondering where Jack was. A horn beeped and she looked out, but that sure wasn't Jack's old Chevy. She frowned deeper when the window opened and his grinning face appeared.

She hurried outside and said, "Jack, whose is this? Is it yours? Did you buy a new car?!"

"Nope. I bought two. One for me, and one for you, baby."

She blinked, her hand covering her stomach as she whispered, "Two? You bought two cars?"

"This one is for you," he said, getting out to hug her to his side. "If you don't like the color we can pick out one you like, but I remember you mentioned you liked this color when we saw it on the road."

"A Cadillac? You got me a Cadillac?" Her voice was two octaves higher with shock. Not that the car wasn't beautiful. It was shimmering silver in the glow of the lights from the diner. "Oh, Jack, it's new?!"

He laughed and hugged her tighter, "Of course it's new, baby. Happy Lottery Win," he teased. "Get in. See how it feels to sit behind the wheel of a real car."

"But, I'm dirty. I stink like grease. Oh, Jack..." She still couldn't believe what she was seeing. "Are you sure we should do this? We don't even have the money yet."

Mighty Fine

"We could buy every car on the lot if we wanted, Ree. Get in. It's fine. I want you to feel the leather, it's amazing."

She slid into the car, her heart racing a mile a minute. She sat there with her hands on her chest, afraid to smudge anything.

"Turn the key, babe and listen to that engine." She did so, on automatic pilot, yet still in shock.

"Listen to that engine, Ree, it purrs."

She nodded, trying to find a voice to ask how much it cost.

"I got a new Ram truck ... ruby red," Jack beamed.

She blinked up at him, starting to tremble. "We shouldn't be so crazy with the money, Jack. We don't even have it yet."

"Didn't I tell you to leave that to me," he grinned. "I found an advisor tonight. His name is George. Sounds real good. I'm going to meet with him tomorrow at nine."

"George? Did you check out his credentials?" Her eyes were on the dash, the lights reminding her of Christmas somehow... but soft and somehow terrifying. She wondered what all those buttons were for and if she'd ever figure them all out.

"Yes, Ree, don't worry. Come on...let's get home."

When he started around the car she slid to the passenger side, beating him to it. He frowned and she said, "You drive. I don't want to wreck it."

He rolled his eyes but went back around to drive, talking about the good life all the way home.

Rita could barely comprehend anything he said, the sound system filling the car with music. The car really was beyond beautiful, but it intimidated her. So elegant...and the only new car she'd ever owned. Not that they actually owned it. You needed the money to own something. Jack kept forgetting that.

Seeing the new truck when home, only served to present her with another sleepless night. At this rate, she doubted she'd ever sleep again.

The next morning Jack was up and out to meet with George, leaving her to her own devices. Normally Rita would run over to Tina's and they'd have coffee together, but she was afraid to. She knew she'd end up telling her about the win and then Jack would have a fit because the lawyer warned them not to tell a soul. But Tina was her best friend and she ached to tell her. She longed to have someone to talk to about all her fears. Jack didn't seem to understand how overwhelming it was to have a brand new expensive car, not to mention the truck, both of which were bought before they even saw the money. If anything happened, their credit would be ruined.

She looked around the kitchen and bit her lip. They'd often talked about remodeling it one day, and when Jack came home, she'd mention maybe doing that when they got their money. It would be a good investment. Their house was really the only thing of value they had.

After his meeting with George, Jack phoned home. When Rita answered he said, "It's all taken care of Rita. I hired him."

Mighty Fine

"You did?"

"Yeah. You should see his office. It's like something in a movie. All stainless steel and glass." She heard the distinct sound of dishes in the background just as he said, "Hey, here he comes now. We're going to lunch to go over a few things. Just wanted you to know so you didn't worry."

"But...well..." She was going to say she wished he'd just come home to tell her what was going on, but sighed. "You won't be too long, right?"

"No, I don't imagine so, hon. I'm in a country club! He must have called ahead to get me in. Who'd a thought, huh?" She heard him say, "George...over here..." Then a simple,

"See you later."

Before she could even say goodbye, he was gone.

As lunches go, Rita thought, this one was epic. It was nearly six by the time Jack got back, looking a bit tipsy and talking a lot louder than usual. "You should have seen that place, Ree. Actually, you will be! We just became members."

"Of a country club?" She couldn't think of anything that would impress her less.

"Yep. George seemed to know everyone in the joint. He introduced me to a few guys there. All big wigs."

She frowned when he stood there holding his fists over top of one another to draw his arms back and swing them low. "I'm going to take up golf!"

Linda Voelker

"How much did you have to drink?"

He laughed and said, "Enough to make me order clubs that were measured and made just for me. Hey, do you want a set too?"

"No. Absolutely not." She sounded as appalled as she felt. Jack golfing? That was just crazy.

He was still grinning as he said, "So, what did you do today?"

She couldn't remember a thing, proving how stunned she was over this side of Jack. "I made lasagna," she offered. "Jack? Do you really think we'll even go to a country club? I mean, isn't there monthly dues or something involved in that?"

He laughed like she'd just told the best joke ever. "Money isn't an issue, Ree. And you and I have lived a lifetime paying dues. It's time to live a little!"

"Well, I was thinking we could remodel the kitchen," Rita said, wanting to remind him of sensible ways they could use the money. "We'd talked about it before but money was tight. Maybe we can look into that when we get the money?"

"Remodel this dump? No way. We're going to move into a new house. Maybe build one!" As he sauntered to the stairs, he said, "I got the name of his travel agent too. After my shower we can plan our first trip."

Rita sank back on the sofa and felt as if the air had been sucked from the room. She didn't know what to think of Jack or his exuberance for lofty things. It only served to make her fear if winning the lottery would ultimately come at too high a price.

3

Rita pulled up to their new house six months later, sitting in the drive to drink it all in. It was hard to believe that it was actually theirs. They'd moved in about three months ago and while Rita did miss the old neighborhood, she loved the four bedroom, stone structure in front of her.

    So many things changed after the win. They'd paid off all their bills with a flourish, in fact, their families as well. Giving Dave and Tina money was an easy joint decision, and after a hard fought battle, the gift was finally accepted. Rita would never forget how choked up Tina had been. It was a testimony to their friendship though, how thrilled they'd been for Jack and Rita.

    Dave frowned, still sure they were being pranked about the win. "Are you pulling my leg?"

    Jack laughed and echoed him, "No, I'm not pulling your leg."

    He then pulled out a card that Rita had found on the value of friendship and handed it to him. Inside was twenty five thousand dollars, which promptly caused a battle royal. It went on for the next five minutes before Rita looked at Tina and whispered, "Please take it?"

    She studied Rita for a moment, then snatched the envelope from Dave, who was still trying to give it back to Jack. Tina hugged Rita again, bursting into tears herself. "If our roof hadn't started leaking," she choked out, "I wouldn't even consider it. Thank you…"

She then hugged Jack and whispered, "Thank you so much."

Dave had choked out a laugh, giving Jack a man-hug so tight it was amazing he didn't crack his spine. "This calls for a celebration! I say we hit Vito's…and you get the tab!"

Of all the ways they might have celebrated, Vito's Pizza place was the absolute best way. That night they stayed till the workers simply began shutting down, talking and laughing and sharing their dreams for the future. A future that Tina and Dave would always be part of.

But they hadn't seen them since the day they'd helped them move in.

It wasn't an intentional thing, but decorating their new home, meeting with the financial adviser that Jack decided on, and trying to adapt to their new lives, time just flew by. The calls between got lost in the shuffle.

And then, there was all that mail.

People came out of the woodwork sending heartbreaking letters of financial need. When Jack came home one day a month after the win, to find her in tears, he knew he had to put a stop to it.

"Rita, honey, look at me." When she did, holding a stack of the ones that were most heart wrenching, he softly said, "Most of the letters here are fabrications, honey. People wanting to get free money any way they can. You'll have yourself sick if you keep this up."

Mighty Fine

"But, Jack...this one says their little boy has cancer and they can't get treatment because his parents are out of work..."

He listened to her choke out a few more stories before he simply took the envelopes and set them aside, gathering her close. "We'll go over charities tonight, hon. You can pick ones that you feel most strongly about, but no more letter reading. Okay?"

She sniffled and gave a slow nod, knowing she would probably have just as hard a time deciding which charity was more deserving. Her emotions were like a roller coaster these days.

Rita and Jack did contribute substantial amounts to five charities and he had been right. It did make her feel better to know that their win would definitely help others.

Realizing how long she was sitting in the car, she decided to get out before the neighbors started to wonder. Reaching into the car her muscles protested, thanks to the gym memberships Jack had purchased for both of them.

"Ohhhhhhhh...so now I am chubby," she'd teased the day he came in so excited about their joint membership. It hadn't been that long ago that he'd assured her the extra twenty she'd gained over the years just made him love snuggling with her all the more.

"I didn't say you were chubby, honey. But we want to be healthy and lead a long, happy life...right?"

So, she went to the gym and even had a personal trainer named Chaz. He was much younger, very muscular, and could have been a model on one of those romance novel covers she once read.

Her hair was now cut and styled in a very fancy salon. They served wine with fresh fruit and cheeses. It was nothing like Cost Cutters at all. And where at first she felt uncomfortable, over time, she came to enjoy those Cinderella moments of feeling so pampered.

Heading inside, she kicked off her Jimmy Choo's and smiled, seeing Jack out on the deck. She loved the layout of this house. Everything was wide open and unhindered by walls. From the front of the house she could see the back, and she found the feel of the openness uplifting. The furnishings were just as light and airy, though she was a nervous wreck for the first month, fearing she'd spill something and stain it. Jack finally broke her from her habit. It hadn't been easy though.

Sliding the glass door open she stepped out to hug him from behind as he talked on the phone. He absently gave her hands a pat, saying, "The stocks made that much? Awesome! That's great, George!"

She should have known, Rita thought. If George were a female, she'd be jealous of all the time the two of them spent either together or on the phone.

As he continued his conversation, she looked out over the yard, thinking it looked like something out of Town and Country magazine. The lawn was pristine and the shrubbery was trimmed by the gardeners each week. They put in a pond with koi fish and lily pads, with a bench Rita loved sitting on to watch them swim.

Her attention went back to Jack when she heard him say,

Mighty Fine

"Why don't you and Crystal come over for dinner Friday? Sure, we can celebrate the stock's success," he grinned.

Rita turned to look his way, seeing his wink, knowing he was aware they weren't on her top ten list of people to spend time with. It wasn't that she had anything specific against George. But she felt on edge around him, which Jack found ridiculous. Even after the fundraising fiasco.

"Good, good. We'll see you around seven then. Bye now, buddy."

He pocketed his phone, keeping his smile, "Buy out all the stores?"

"You invited George and Crystal to dinner?"

"A little financial celebration, Rita." He moved in to kiss her forehead. "Did you leave anything for others to buy, or do they have to restock?"

She bit back a sigh, for it was clear he was trying to divert the conversation. "We were just with them a week ago, remember? We went to that boring political dinner where we had to pay thousands of dollars to eat raw meat."

Looking at her with exaggerated patience, he sighed. "It was a fundraiser and tax deductible. So it's a good thing." He shook his head and added, "I don't know what your problem is with George. He's a smart guy, Rita. I learn a lot from him."

"He's nothing like Dave."

Jack looked confused for a moment before he realized who she meant. "True. But we aren't in the old neighborhood anymore, Rita. We're in the big leagues now."

He went inside, those words his parting comment. She didn't like the sound of those words, but they echoed in her head anyway.

"So," she countered, following him inside, "we're in the big leagues?" She scurried to get ahead of him, blocking his path, "What does that mean exactly?"

Jack sighed, knowing he'd misspoken. "We hit the lottery, Rita. That's all. It put us in a different social class." He spoke as if he were talking to a three year old and it ticked her off.

Her temper started to make itself known. "Oh, and what are Dave and Tina now? The little people? The peasants?"

Rita knew she was overreacting, but she couldn't help it. It was as if all those little things that had changed so subtly had just become clear.

Jack took in her narrowed eyes and sighed, not wanting an argument. He didn't understand why he was always feeling a need to explain himself to her. "You know exactly what I meant and I'm not in the mood for you to start dissecting everything I say. George and Crystal will be here Friday for dinner. Call that caterer from the club. Order for four ... the lobster bisque."

She was still ready for battle but he walked around her to leave throug the front door, which closed none too gently behind him. She let out a growl of frustration and paced. Who did he think he was? No, who did he think she was? Where did he get off at, telling her to call the caterer like she was his underling?

She finally plopped down on the couch and sighed. Her worst fear the night they'd won sure seemed to be surfacing. The money

Mighty Fine

had changed Jack. Then again, thinking of all her shopping trips, she had to admit it changed her as well. The realization made her heart heavy.

The changes were so subtle at first that she barely took note. But 'only the best' had become the new mantra. They once appreciated everything so much more. Finding a sale was exciting or something in their size on a clearance rack. Rita remembered scanning the food store ads for specials, like the ten for ten's on tuna or can goods. Now they didn't even buy canned goods. It was fresh...pricey...the best.

Rita sat up and dashed at a tear that slid free. She'd call Tina. No matter what happened in either of their lives, they always felt better after a talk. Taking her cell phone from her purse, she called her old friend, but it went to voice mail. Knowing that Tina never went anywhere without her cell, Rita felt a pang of sadness. Tina must be screening her calls and Rita's was now one she didn't want to take. She couldn't blame her.

"Hey, girlie...it's me, Rita. Just wanted to call and see how you guys are. I miss you."

She ended it there, afraid she'd cry. How could something as wonderful as winning the lottery, leave her feeling so alone?

Rita grabbed her bags and went up to their bedroom, no longer as tickled with her new clothes. She took the designer dress from the bag and looked at it with new eyes. She'd been so thrilled to think she would own a dress designed by the one that clothed so many stars, that she almost ran to the cashier. Picking up the receipt to check the price she felt ill. She'd paid more than their old mortgage and utility bills for three months combined and where would she ever wear it?

She thrust it onto the rack in her walk-in closet and looked around at all the things she now owned. Her shoes were impressive. All of them left her learning to walk all over again. She used to buy cheap sneakers at Walmart and loved them. Levi was her designer of choice. Jack was right, she'd moved up to the big league with him.

Feeling so ashamed, she showered, but it did nothing to wash away her guilt.

Jack couldn't figure out the change in Rita. You'd think she'd be so happy about never having to worry about money again, that she'd be bouncing off the walls. But no, not Rita. That excitement she'd felt at first, seemed to shift into guilt of some kind. Her first big purchase after the win was a purse from Target. Even at that, she felt she'd paid too much. It's funny, but her being so careful about money was great when they had none, but those days were behind them. He had to teach her how to spend. How crazy was that?

He smirked, realizing he didn't really have to do that so much anymore. She'd found her footing in elite shops lately. The night of the political dinner with George, she looked stunning. He'd booked a flight to New York, her dress was bought there. Of course, there weren't tags on the dresses. That seemed to help until the sale was rung up. She went pale and threw up once back

Mighty Fine

in the hotel.

Tonight was the night that George and Crystal would be coming, and he knew she wasn't happy with that. Maybe she was right. He did spend a lot of time connected to George. It was just that he had vowed after the win that they'd never struggle again. He wanted to make sure the money would last and he needed it to work for them. George seemed to know his stuff. He also knew a lot of people that were important and gave him the introductions needed for this new social realm. Rita was just struggling to accept the changes, but they weren't bad changes. She just needed to adjust.

Deciding to stop at the jewelers, he bought her a pair of diamond earrings. It was something he never could have done a year ago, but she deserved the best. Maybe wearing them tonight would make dining with George a little more bearable.

He imagined her all spruced up in their new home with a warm smile on her pretty face as she welcomed their guests. And oddly, she would welcome them. That was just the way Rita was. She treated everyone like they were old friends and would give them whatever she could if it would help them out. He knew how lucky he was to have her in his life. They rarely fought and always talked things out. She forgave him for everything and many times over. Smiling, he knew everything would be fine. It always was. He pulled into the driveway before heading inside to find her.

Rita was in the kitchen, humming to the radio as she put the finishing touches on the salad. She'd made a huge pot of sauce and had the meatballs in the oven. She decided to make Jack's favorite meal and knew in her heart, he'd love it. She even baked peach pies...another favorite of Jack's.

"Hey, Rita, are you down here?"

She smiled, glad he was home. "I'm in the kitchen, Jack."

He joined her, but his smile faded as he noticed the big pot on the stove "Is that spaghetti sauce? Did you forget we're having company?"

Rita moved around the island to hug him. "Nope, I didn't forget and yep...it's sauce."

Jack pulled back, his frown deepening. "I told you to call for the lobster bisque."

"I know, babe, but I decided to make your favorite meal instead. You know I love to cook."

Earrings and nostalgia quickly forgotten, his eyes darkened, "Is this really how you think we're going to live our lives? With you deliberately going against everything I say?"

She looked at him, her expression a blend of hurt and defensiveness. "I'm not going against you. I wanted to surprise you. What's the problem, Jack?"

As that had been what he'd wondered, his tone was a bit sharper than he realized. "That's what I want to know, Rita. Look around you and tell me what problems you have. You have a new house, new car, a closet full of clothes and shoes--and enough jewelry to choke a horse, and yet you refuse to have the dinner I requested. Are you out to prove a point, Rita? Is that why you're wearing those ratty jeans and a t-shirt? Is that how you plan

Mighty Fine

to look when our company comes?" He cocked his head, eyes flashing, "You want to shame me, is that it?"

She was so stunned by his tirade, she could do no more than blink. But then, her pain shifted to anger. "Shame you? I shame you, Jack? Isn't that funny," she mused sarcastically. "You used to say you were proud of me. You didn't care that I wore jeans and a t-shirt. You loved me for me." She looked at him, her eyes flashing. "I don't even know who you are anymore."

Maybe it was seeing how she differed from the woman he had just been thinking about that had him stand straighter and back off. Whatever it was, for the first time ever, he knew the respect she once had for him was gone and he wasn't too crazy about her either. He dropped the earrings on the counter. "You serve whatever you want, but if you're still in those jeans when I come out of the shower, I'll take our company to the club for dinner."

Shocked by that decree, Rita watched him disappear from her view. She looked at the box on the counter and opened it with shaking hands, the two perfectly shaped diamond hearts only making a mockery of her own breaking heart.

Forty minutes later when Jack rejoined her, she was in linen slacks and a blouse, but neither of them spoke. The earrings however, lay open on the counter, speaking volumes.

"You're so quiet tonight, Rita," George boomed in his loud voice. "You aren't coming down with anything are you?"

She glanced his way with what she hoped was a smile. "No, I have just been listening, trying to learn from the conversation. I know absolutely nothing about the market."

He dabbed his mouth with his napkin, grinning at her. "You don't have to worry your head about that. I'm teaching your husband everything I know. Great meal, by the way. I haven't had spaghetti and meatballs this good since we went to Antonio's. Did you have them cater?"

Jack chuckled dryly, "No way. Rita wanted to show off her own culinary talent. This is all her doing. She even baked homemade pies." He couldn't help but add, "Guess you can take the girl out of the middle class, you just can't take the middle class out of the girl."

The minute he made the joke, he wished he hadn't. George laughed his head off, but Jack couldn't miss the way Rita flinched.

She regained her voice enough to say, "This used to be Jack's favorite meal...but his tastes have changed." She stood, picking up her plate that was barely touched. "I'll go put on fresh coffee. Peach pie anyone?"

As Rita gathered up their plates, Crystal, a tall, thin redhead with heavy makeup, whined, "Oh, I couldn't. Too many carbs and they all go to my hips."

George, true to his crass form, leaned back to look at her bottom as it perched on the chair. "Too late to worry now, baby doll."

The plates started to rattle in her hand, covered by that mocking laugh George had, and she quickly moved to the kitchen.

Mighty Fine

She literally trembled with all she was feeling. How could Jack possibly see George so differently? Was George really the one Jack wanted to be like? Did he want her to become like Crystal?

She couldn't help but remember the night of the fundraiser. George had been so rude to the waitress that Rita was sickened by it. Having worked in the diner for years, she knew it wasn't the easiest job to begin with, and their waitress looked to be close to sixty. "I told you five minutes ago to bring me coffee! Is there a problem with your ability to do your job?"

"No, sir," she managed to say, a pained smile on her face.

"I'll get it for you now."

"She's working a large section," Rita had said gently, wanting to point that out in case he'd missed the fact.

"She's working to serve me," he countered with a scowl.

"And doing a piss poor job of it."

Crystal didn't help. "She's a little long in the tooth for the position. She should be feeding pigeons in the park by now."

George found her comment amusing and Rita had stiffened.

Jack had placed a hand on her thigh and she knew he did that to calm her, but when the waitress returned with the coffee, George snapped, "I'll take some of that chocolate torte...and see if you can get it to me before it grows stale."

That was the night she decided there was little to like about George and Crystal.

Jack was never rude to anyone, but if he continued to look at George as a role model, it wouldn't be long before he'd think like him, act like him, and be like him. The thought knotted her stomach.

She tried to stop her thoughts as she made coffee, but they kept coming in spite of it. They may not have had money before, but they had each other. There was nothing they couldn't face or overcome together and they were happy in spite of it all.

She struggled to swallow past the lump in her throat, unaware that Jack had joined her till he spoke softly. "Rita? You okay?"

Turning slowly she looked up at him, her eyes shimmering. "Do you love me?"

Regretting his impulse to check on her, he frowned.

"Really? Now?"

She turned away again, his refusal to simply say 'yes' filling her with a sharp pain. He turned her to cup her chin, forcing her to look at him. When he spoke, his voice was soothing. "Rita...Two happily married people happened to win the lottery. It shouldn't change things negatively, right? We just have the means to live beyond our wildest expectations." He kissed her forehead and stepped back, patting her linen clad bottom. "I came in to tell you Crystal decided she will have a piece of pie. To spite George, I'm thinking," he winked.

While it wasn't exactly a declaration of undying love, it was a small glimpse of the old Jack. That was what helped her get a grip. She turned to get the plates, turning back to find he'd gone. Whispering a prayer that she'd get through the rest of the evening, she cut the pie and served their guests, her smile forced, perhaps, but there.

"Great meal," George decided, using his fork to catch the

Mighty Fine

pie crust crumbs on his plate. "Crystal can't cook for crap."

Crystal countered in her aloof way. "Perhaps if you were skin and bones—which you're far from—people would buy that."

Rita mentally gave her two points, glad she got in a dig as Jack ran his hand over her back and smiled. "It was a great dinner, Rita."

She smiled back at him gratefully. She knew he could have left it unsaid after their earlier tiff, so it meant a lot. "I'm glad you enjoyed it."

George burped and leaned forward, "I wanted to talk with you about investing in a social site on the web. It took a dive, but it's bound to climb again...."

Rita, not really interested in such things, glanced at Crystal as George droned on. "That's a pretty necklace."

Fingering it, Crystal offered a cool smile. "Yes, I had it custom made. I love emeralds and these are flawless." She studied Rita's hand as she took a sip of coffee. "Why didn't you have Jack get you a new ring set? You can surely afford something more than what you have." She leaned a bit forward too, adding, "It screams cheap, if you want my opinion."

Rita felt her face flame, knowing the top of her head was about to explode. "Well, in my book, Crystal, sentiment means more than flash," she replied in a strained tone. "I happen to love my wedding set and could care less what your opinion is!" She couldn't believe she'd let that one come out.

Jack had caught the gist of the conversation, but George obviously hadn't. "Calm down, Rita," he laughed. "Did you have too much coffee, or what?"

She would have lunged across the table to slug him if Jack hadn't said, "No..." He was looking at Crystal who looked mildly surprised by Rita's attack, as she'd refer to it from then on. "It was all I could afford at the time, though if I could have, I'd have given her the Hope diamond." He held Rita's hand, giving it a soft, reassuring squeeze. "And I did offer to buy her a new set after the win. She wouldn't hear of it, which says a lot about her."

Struggling to focus on Jack's praise and not her need to throw them out of their home, she looked at him. "My rings mean the world to me. They signify our love."

"Hear that, Crystal? Why can't you be more like that? It would save me a ton of dough."

Ignoring him, Rita added, "I do have beautiful jewelry that Jack bought for me, by the way. I just don't wear it every day. I don't want anything to happen to it."

Crystal sounded bored. "Insure it, Rita. Anything happens, just replace it. Everything is replaceable."

Curious now, Rita asked, "But doesn't your jewelry from George hold meaning for you? Doesn't it remind you of a special memory of the reason for it?"

"Let's not go there," George snorted. "Crystal will start wanting me to celebrate things I always forget."

"After twelve years, he still doesn't know my birthday," Crystal sighed.

"But I do know you're getting old," he retorted. "Time to trade you in for a newer model."

Mighty Fine

Rita stood to clear the table, knowing she had better leave the room before she said something she might regret. Might being the operative word. She doubted she'd regret it one single bit.

She slammed the dishes in the sink, knowing when Jack joined her, that it was overheard. "Rita, it doesn't concern you. Just relax."

She spun, her eyes flashing. "He's crass...arrogant...and rude!" she hissed quietly. "I don't like him and she's no better."

"They are our guests." His whisper was harsh, matching what hers had been. "Their behavior shouldn't influence yours."

She poked his chest with a finger, "And you should call him on it. You shouldn't let him act that way in our house!" His earlier comment still in the back of her mind she added, "Unless that's too middle class for you now."

There's a time and place for everything. The heat of the moment isn't the best time to add fuel to the fire and she regretted it seeing his reaction. He stood straighter, his jaw clenching. "I guess I was hoping you'd be a little more like the woman I married, than this sad, vindictive one you've become."

She struggled to catch her breath, his words hitting the mark as he went back to the dining room. Had she become that way? No, she told herself. It was Jack that changed! She sniffled, rinsing the dishes, praying she wouldn't cry. She was going to have to face them again, and she couldn't cry. She wasn't one of those pretty criers on TV. Her eyes puffed shut and she got all blotchy.

"Hey, Rita..." George called out. "you go down the garbage

Linda Voelker

disposal or what?"

Closing her eyes and counting to ten, she swallowed hard and rejoined them.

By the time they left it was nearly midnight and Rita's head was pounding. When she went to say as much to Jack, he said, "I don't want to hear a word, Rita. I'm tired. Goodnight."

And once again, Rita struggled with the way things had changed.

.

4

Jack found himself driving around the next day with no destination in mind. He just wanted to be anywhere but home. It wasn't that he didn't love Rita. It was that he couldn't understand her. Being around her when she was so ready to pounce on him was something new. Something he never expected from her. They'd never been the arguing type.

He went to a local driving range to practice his game, knowing he needed a lot of practice. It wasn't lost on him that golf wasn't something he enjoyed. He only did it because everyone in his new circle of friends golfed.

He hit a few line drives that were off center, realizing the term 'friends' was off too. They weren't his friends in the same sense that Dave and had been. Hell, Dave was one of those guys that would drop everything to come over to help when asked. Sometimes even without his asking. Like when that storm hit a few years back and knocked their tree down in the front yard. It was Dave that came over with his power saw and had most of it taken care of before Jack even got home from work. He couldn't imagine George doing anything like that.

"Jack? Is that really you?"

Knowing that voice, he turned to see Connie Tyler, the woman he'd been dating for years when he'd met Rita...and boy, did she look good. Her auburn hair was long and thick, her green eyes sparkled in the sunlight.

"Connie?" She'd hugged him warmly before pulling back to grin up at him as he smiled. "What are you doing here?"

She laughed and gave a nod toward a guy that was paying for their buckets of balls. "I'm with Emerson, what a name, huh?"

Jack glanced at the man with salt and pepper hair and felt a slight twinge of jealousy, which was crazy. He looked back at Connie as she added, "I met him a few months ago at a baseball game. He's an okay guy, but--" she shrugged, and Jack sensed the last of that sentence was 'he isn't like you' and felt placated. "Hey...congrats! I heard you won the big one."

Jack laughed softly, "Yeah, who'd a thunk it, huh?"

"I'm glad you did, Jack. Nobody deserves it more than you." She reached up to straighten the collar of his golf shirt, which he wore now. It was something that he wouldn't have worn back when they were together. The gesture wasn't meant to be anything more than that, but it brought back a time when they were closer. "I hear you live up on the hill now. Imagine you, rich and living high on the hog," she teased.

Emerson joined them, a polite, but bored smile on his face. "Oh," Connie smiled, stepping away to introduce them. "Emerson...this is Jack...Jack, Emerson. Jack was a close friend of mine for a long time," she added softly, but there was a shift in tone that Jack remembered as well. He liked the memory.

"Nice to meet you," Emerson said, shifting his pail to his left hand to offer his right. Upon contact with Jack's extended

Mighty Fine

hand, he said, "Constance, I have a meeting at one. If we want to hit these balls, we'll need to move on."

Her big hazel eyes lifted to Jack's. "It was so great seeing you, Jack. Give me a call sometime so we can catch up."

Jack gave a nod, watching them turn to walk away, lost in memories he'd long since forgotten. They all came back though, just that quickly. As did her phone number. He frowned, hitting the ball from the tee in a perfect line drive.

Rita sat on the bench in the backyard, watching the colorful fish swim slowly around the pond. She sipped her coffee, lost in thought. Jack woke before she had that morning, and when she heard the drawer of the dresser slide, she woke to silently watch him dress. Any other morning she'd have whispered his name, patted the bed and they would have started the day out much differently than in that strained silence it had. Lately, that soft current of tension was the norm.

She didn't even ask him where he was off to. It didn't seem to matter.

After he left she'd done her usual cleaning, dusting and running the vacuum cleaner, trying to still her thoughts by blasting the music that usually had her singing along off key. Today it seemed as if every song was a love song and none of them made her feel better. She'd even gone through the paper, clipping coupons...but that fell flat as well. She didn't need to use them anymore. They made her feel nostalgic for the good old days.

She wondered where Jack was at, though she knew he was probably with George. Rita stood, looking in the pond to see a baby koi fish dart from under a lily pad and smiled. It was so tiny, but by next year, would blend in with the rest. The analogy swallowed her smile. She felt like that little fish swimming in too big a pond.

As she walked across the yard toward the house, she heard the garage door open next door. She stopped to wave at the woman, who clearly saw her, but didn't bother to respond in any way. She just went into the garage and pulled out a moment later in her Porsche, pulling up the driveway as the door automatically closed behind her.

Feeling smaller than the new baby fish, Rita went back into the house.

Jack came home to find Rita going through photo albums, moving to sit beside her on the couch. More in need to remember the love he had for her, and stop dwelling on memories of Connie. Perhaps a bit of guilt was all it took. He'd called Connie and left a message on her phone saying it was good to see her again. He now wished he hadn't been so impulsive.

"Remember this?" Rita was pointing to a photo of Jack in a top hat, a goofy grin on his face. "We had so much fun at that party."

It was at Dave and Tina's house. They'd thrown a party one

Mighty Fine

year for Presidents Day...any excuse for a get together.

He chuckled, "I do. Remember how the smoker blew up that night? I thought Tina was going to kill Dave for not remembering to check it."

Rita giggled, "I know, but by the end of the night, she was in his white Washington wig and he was fluttering that fan she'd carried."

Jack was still grinning. "It looked like an M-80 had gone off in his yard."

Rita felt the need to flip back to the beginning of the album. "Look at us, Jack. We were on our honeymoon. I still remember the Asian couple that took this picture."

His arm draped around her shoulders as he snorted. "Who wouldn't? It's rare to find Asian people staying in a cabin of a campground."

They'd decided to just go away for a weekend honeymoon, not too far from home. They'd wanted to use the money for a down payment on their old home. It made more sense not to blow money on some big trip. Besides, they'd been so happy it didn't matter where they went. They were too busy celebrating their love.

"They were so sweet."

Jack flipped the page and wished he hadn't. It showed Rita beaming, holding up the pregnancy test that said they were expecting a baby. He remembered the devastation they'd both felt a few weeks later when she miscarried. He tried to turn the page before she noticed the photo too, but she stilled his hand.

Linda Voelker

"No, Jack...it's okay. I just sorry that we didn't have children, that I couldn't carry one."

He took the album and set it aside, shifting her onto his lap. She curled up there, resting her head on his shoulder.

"I felt bad when we lost the baby too, Ree. But I don't feel that not having children took anything away from us. I can't imagine me without you."

Rita ran her hand over his chest. "You would have been such a great dad. I always thought we'd have a houseful of little ones."

She peeked up at him and slowly smiled, remembering her discovery. Coming to her feet she tugged his hand. "Come with me, Jack. I have to show you something!"

He frowned, but stood, eyes twinkling. "What?"

"We do have a baby. I just noticed it this morning..."

He knew when she slid the sliding glass doors open, the baby was in the pond. Chuckling over her excitement, he followed. His cell phone buzzed along the way, and he pulled it out and recognized the old, familiar number.

"I'll be right there, babe. I have to take this..."

And in that split second, he set himself up to risk everything, but couldn't resist taking the call.

That evening when Jack said he was meeting George for a dinner meeting, Rita didn't think much about it. He did that with George. But she knew Jack and something wasn't right. While

Mighty Fine

they'd been so at ease moments before his cell phone rang, when he finally joined her at the pond, he was distracted. His smile seemed a bit forced as she pointed out the fish and gushed over it. He barely reacted before he mentioned the meeting and went inside to change. When he came back downstairs he wouldn't even look at her and that's when she felt uneasy. It was like he was hiding something. He'd always been in charge of the money so maybe something was wrong there. Maybe George just told him they'd lost money in the stock.

"Where are you meeting George," she asked.

"His office and we'll go from there."

He grabbed his keys and was heading to the door when she spoke, "Jack, it's only money. Okay?"

He paused, wondering what she meant by that. Realizing she mistook his almost tangible guilt as money problems, he gave a nod, "See you later...don't wait up, Ree. I don't know how late I'll be."

From the moment he left the house, he fought a mental war with himself. He knew he shouldn't be meeting Connie. Knew no good would come of it. But then, he told himself, they were 'old friends' just as she'd claimed when introducing him to that guy she was with. Friends they were and friends they would remain. But you can't be with someone for close to three years and not wonder how they are. He'd been like one of her family back then, and he was curious how they were too. That's what he decided to latch onto. It was just a way to find out and move on.

He pulled into the lot of the Italian Oven they used to frequent and saw her step out of a red jeep, smiling wide and waving. She did look good, even after all these years.

Hugging him, she admitted, "I wasn't sure you'd really come, Jack. I'm glad you did."

Rita came to his mind, one last chance to step back, but he found himself saying, "Me, too. Let's go find a table."

Rita was in bed when he returned, unable to sleep. When he came in she sat up and offered a smile. "Some meeting, babe. I'll bet you're beat."

Again, not meeting her gaze, he undressed and said, "Yeah, I am." He had replayed what he'd say to explain the late hour all the way home, none of that came from his lips though. "I ran into an old friend. I'll tell you about it in the morning." He crawled into bed and kissed her softly on the forehead. "Night, Ree."

She said nothing, her nose picking up a soft scent of White Diamonds. He settled in on his side, back to her and silence reigned.

Maybe it wasn't about money. Could he be cheating on her? Rita rolled to her side and pushed the thought from her mind. He wouldn't do that. Not Jack. But something wasn't right. She spend the rest of the night wondering what it could be.

Mighty Fine

By morning, Rita had found a million reasons why Jack might have that scent on him. The rich weren't any less heavy handed with perfume than others. He'd probably just hugged someone from that meeting. The scent clung to him because of that. Her Gramma used to have a saying about not letting trouble, trouble you until trouble really gave you reason. She was sure she was doing just that. Borrowing trouble where there was none.

She'd made French toast while Jack was in the shower, smiling at him when he joined her, hair still damp and tousled. "Perfect timing," she smiled, setting his plate down. "So what's on the agenda today?"

He sat, smiling at the plate rather than her. "Nothing too much," he picked up the syrup and drizzled it over the top of the stack. "Thought I'd go hit some balls at the range." He didn't add that he was to meet Connie at ten.

"Maybe I'll go too," she smiled, settling in her chair to sip her coffee. "I used to like miniature golf."

He thought fast, adding, "Well, afterward, I'm going to take the truck to have the detail work done. Let's plan on going to hit balls another day, Ree. Mmmm...this is good."

"So," she said, trying to shake her disappointment. "Who did you run into last night?"

Jack hesitated a beat too long, then casually said, "Oh... Connie."

Rita knew about Connie. She remembered feeling bad that her gain was another woman's loss, even though it was a brief feeling at the time. Hoping her tone remained neutral she asked, "Where was the dinner? Was she there alone?"

"The Magpie...and no, with a man." He took a sip of coffee and set it back down with a shrug. "I was surprised to run into her. It's been a while."

Rita shifted on the chair, different emotions struggling for top billing. "So, what did she have to say? Is she married to the man? Did you tell her about the house...the win...?" Me, she wondered without adding it aloud.

"It wasn't more than a polite thing...Hi, how ya doing... you look good..."

He stopped there, looking like he'd said too much, which made Rita ask, "How good?"

He looked at her then. Fully. Clearly annoyed. "Rita, if you're going to make more of it than it was, I'm done talking about it. I don't have all the answers to your inquisition. I just ran into her and that was the end of it."

She watched as he pushed away from the table and wasn't surprised when he grabbed his keys and left. Not surprised, but hurt none the less.

Trouble was making itself known.

5

For the first time in a long time, Rita was relieved when Jack left. She needed time to think. It threw her to know he'd run into Connie, because she knew of their history. She also knew she couldn't let her jealousy show or it would make her look like she was at fault over not trusting him.

She'd never had cause to distrust him before and tried to remember that.

After clearing the dishes from the table and starting the dishwasher, she got the paper from the counter, seeing the earrings still sitting there. Flashes of his happily married couple speech echoed in her thoughts as she gently set the box aside to take the paper to the table.

News was bad no matter where you might live, she decided, the headlines always bold and the words below condemning someone or something. She scanned the front page and found herself leafing through the whole section, a bit distracted and unwilling to admit to herself why.

Rita filled the mug with coffee and added a bit of cream, then turned to the next section. There on the front page was a picture of a man with a huge smile, making Rita smile just looking at it. She settled in to read the article about the man behind the concept of "Shopping in Grace".

Linda Voelker

"Everyone knows that the west side of town isn't the most easy to live in. Poverty is the thread that weaves the community together. Random shootings and crime are the flavor of any given day. But in the midst of it all, stands a man that is not only tall in stature but big in heart. Odis Walker runs the Grace Shop, offering clothing, furniture and even food to the community, wanting only to bring hope where so many found none. "I can't say that I'm anyone special," he modestly commented when we interviewed him. "The Good Book is pretty clear about our purpose in this life. We're meant to help one another and we believe that here. Folks give what they no longer want or need and I just spruce it up for the ones that do." Looking around the shop I couldn't help but think of things that were in my garage to be trashed, like an old bed frame and a stereo that was on the fritz. When I mentioned them to Odis he offered me that smile that made me glad I had the chance to meet him. "That would be mighty fine, Miss Rose. If you drop it off, we'll have use of it." When I got back in the car to return to the paper to print this article, that's exactly how I felt. Mighty fine!"

Rita read the article again, and then grabbed a pen to jot down the name and number of the church that was given, feeling some excitement that she missed. Running up to change, she took the dress from the closet, glad she hadn't lost the receipt, with a new mission in mind.

Connie wore jeans, remembering how Jack always liked her

Mighty Fine

in them. Her mango pullover and hoop earrings completed the casual look, though she was a nervous wreck about seeing him again. Running into him at the range was such a shock, but that faded quickly. So often she'd wondered what she'd say to him if she ever saw him again, but when it happened, she couldn't think of anything, except how good it was to see him again. She knew he was thinking the same by the smile on his face.

But that smile wasn't hers anymore, she reminded herself, brushing her hair yet again. Jack was married. It almost killed her when he actually got married five months after dumping her. Try as she might, she couldn't figure out when he'd stopped loving her. They'd been together so long and had been happy. She knew he was happy because he never complained. It seemed as if everything had been going along just like normal. She remembered how they talked about going to the beach for vacation that summer, then the next day, he mentioned stopping to help a lady that broke down on the highway. She didn't think anything of it, Jack was always stopping to help people. But evidently, Jack thought a lot about it.

As she spritzed perfume on, she tried to calm down. It wasn't like she was in the wrong. If anything, Jack was. Right? She looked at her reflection and exhaled before smiling. "Right," she whispered, grabbing her purse to head out to the car.

With the money tucked in her Gucci bag, Rita found herself driving the streets of the west end, gripping the wheel until her knuckles were white. She was out of her comfort zone and more than a little nervous. Jack would be furious if he knew where she was going. She knew his lecture would be filled with concern about the danger she was putting herself in. Being lost didn't help either.

It was then that she remembered the car had a GPS system and pulling into a gas station, she whispered a prayer that she could figure it out. Twenty minutes later, she was relieved she had. The church was around the corner on the next block.

The church itself needed a bit of paint, the white was peeling from the wooden building. She pulled into the lot that wound to the back and exhaled seeing the wooden sign for The Grace Shop over the back door. Her heart was pounding in her ears as she looked all around to be sure nobody else was there, then she grabbed her purse and all but ran to the door. Opening it, a bell tingled. For some reason 'It's a Wonderful Life' came to mind and she smiled at the thought of one of Clarence's friends getting his wings.

The basement was large, but over flowing with junk. No, second hand things, she mentally corrected. She saw a teenaged girl in the corner, looking at prom dresses, but other than her, nobody was there. She walked in further and felt the young girl's gaze, knowing she was wondering what she was doing there. Rita was starting to wonder herself. "Hello? Mr. Walker? Are you here?"

"Back here, ma'am. Workin' on a washing machine."

The article forgot to mention that along with the man being

Mighty Fine

tall and of big heart, he had a deep, velvety voice, much like Barry White's. Stepping tentatively around boxes of books, she looked up to see a chipped white washing machine with long, jean clad calves and work boots jutting off to the side from the base of it.

"Hi..." Her voice cracked and she cleared her throat. "I just read the article about you in the paper," she explained, her eyes on the boots, "and wanted to donate some money." Rita started riffling through her purse for it, looking up in time to see the crown of his bald head before a pair of kind, deep brown eyes twinkled into view. She held out her fist of bills and blinked as he came to his feet, his grin even brighter than she'd expected.

Glancing at the money then at her flushed face, he chuckled.

"That's a mite more money than our donation box has ever seen, Miss...?"

"R-Rita. I'm Rita Brown."

"Miss Rita," he finished, wiping his hands on his overalls. "The donation box is by the door there," he nodded, indicating the door she'd just entered.

Frowning, she blurted, "But that's a crazy place to have a donation box...." She blushed deeper and stammered, "I...I mean, anyone can just take it and run."

His smile never wavered. "I imagine you're right, Miss Rita. But if they want it that bad, best to keep it there. Saves me from any confrontations."

She lowered her hand and whispered, "Oh. I suppose…"

He looked up at the door as the bell tinkled again, and Rita watched as a weary looking, young woman entered, a baby in her arms, another trailing behind holding the back of her skirt.

"Mornin' Miss Thelma! I was wonderin' where you'd gotten to. Haven't seen you in a week at least."

She smiled and glanced from Odis to Rita. "That your fancy car out there?"

Her heart tripped as she nodded.

"Brave woman to leave it there on its own."

Rita's impulse was to run and save it, but she found herself saying, "I'm sure it will be fine. And if anyone wants it that bad, I better stay put. Saves me from any confrontations."

Odis let out a bark of laughter that soon had Rita smiling as well. Especially when he said, "You and I would be fast friends, Miss Rita...that's for sure." A testimony to his upbringing, he added, "Miss Rita, this is Miss Thelma...and that boy peekin' out from behind her is Marcus. He's the big brother to that baby girl Momma's holding. Her name is Miss Reatha."

"It's nice to meet you, Miss Thelma...you too, Marcus," Rita added as she waved. "You must be so tickled to have such an adorable baby sister."

The boy nodded and hid once more, the adults smiling at his antics.

"Thank you, Miss Rita," Thelma replied, "It's nice to meet you too." Her eyes moved to Odis once more, "Reatha is outgrowing everything she has," Thelma said, jiggling the baby on her hip. "Do you have any baby clothes in?"

"I think we just might. Miss Carla brought in some things

Mighty Fine

just yesterday. I'm pretty sure I have them over here," he said, leading her down a thin aisle between tables.

Rita watched, realizing how fortunate she'd been all of her life. They may not have had much, even when she was growing up, but they'd never been forced to wear clothes from a second hand shop.

She looked around a bit more, holding the door when a man came in carrying a trunk. "Not sure if there's much use for this," he'd said, dropping it in the back of the basement. "Just needs a bit of elbow grease."

Rita smiled, "I'm sure someone will appreciate it. Thank you."

He nodded, heading back to the door and Rita found herself looking around for cleaning supplies. Once she found them, she set her purse down and pocketed the money in her white Prada pants and pushed up her sleeves. Hunkering down she set about using some of that elbow grease needed to clean up the trunk.

It wasn't much later that she realized she had company. Marcus stood there watching, his eyes on the trunk.

"Hey, Marcus..."

"Toys in 'ere?"

She feigned curiosity herself. "Hmmm...I don't know! Maybe there are toys. Or maybe it's a pirate chest filled with treasure!"

The boy shifted foot to foot, clearly excited by the prospect.

Rita pretended to try to open it, grunting as if it were stuck.

"Oh...I need help. Can you help me push the lid up, Marcus?"

Linda Voelker

Nodding, the little boy placed two dimpled hands on the lid next to Rita's. He even grunted for good measure. Rita inched it up slowly, Marcus nearly topping inside as he inspected it.

"Nope...nuthin'," the boy said, his excitement diminished.

"Marcus! You get over here right now and stop bothering Miss Rita!"

Rita couldn't help but hug the boy, standing to say, "He's no bother. He even helped me see if there was anything in the trunk, right, Marcus?"

He nodded, scampering off to join his mother.

Odis had returned to softly chide, "Now look at those pretty slacks, Miss Rita. You're getting them dirty from the muck on that trunk."

Rita glanced down at them and smiled, shrugging. "It's okay. I'm sure it'll come out in the wash. I'm almost done..." She bent back down to her task as Odis watched. "Really," she assured him, "I'm enjoying it."

He chuckled and moved to the washer again. "Who am I to interfere with your enjoyment?"

She peeked back to see Thelma had now moved to a table of shoes, struggling to fit Marcus' feet in a pair of sneakers. Seeing her, Odis softly said, "They've hit a rough patch. Thelma's husband is out of work and not having much luck finding another job."

She caught Odis' eye and nodded to the other side of the basement, glad when he followed her, "I'd like to give them this money, but I don't want to insult her in any way."

Mighty Fine

His eyes were filled with admiration as he looked at her. "Hmm...Why not see if you can find a book in that box for Marcus? I imagine you can find treasure in more places than a dirty old trunk."

She smiled and quickly moved to the box, finding a book of fairy tales. She opened it to the middle and put the money inside, moving back to Odis who was ready with a bag, "That was mighty fine of you, Miss Rita."

She blinked back unexpected tears. "It's really nothing and I'm just glad it will help them out. Marcus is such a precious little boy."

The conversation ended when Thelma was in earshot, holding two outfits for Reatha and a ratty plastic car for Marcus. "If you happen to see a pair of shoes, size three or four, can you set them aside?"

"You bet I will," Odis smiled, placing the things in the bag with the book. "Miss Rita put a special surprise in here for Marcus. Maybe when you get home you can read him a story."

"It's fairy tales...I hope he doesn't have it already," Rita added.

"Fairy tales...they all end in happily ever after," Thelma snorted, "I could use me a good fairy tale ending too."

"Something tells me you just might find one today, Miss Thelma," Odis beamed.

Making a mocking sound, Thelma thanked them and left, Marcus latching onto the material of the back of her skirt to keep pace, clutching the plastic car to his side.

Linda Voelker

Rita quickly moved back to the trunk, not wanting to cry in front of Odis. Life was so unfair. She had so much when others had so little.

Sensing her need to avoid his noticing, he went back to the washing machine and tinkered a bit more. "So, Miss Rita," he said from behind it, "I take it you're not from around here."

She let out a choked laugh, saying, "No, I'm from the south hills, but we just moved there a few months ago. We hit the lottery."

Odis was grinning, you could hear it in his voice. "That's a wonderful thing, Miss Rita. It's nice to hear that good things happen to good people." He stood, patting the washer. "There... good as new."

Rita worked to remove a caked on area of filth and sighed, "Money is nice, but it's not everything I once thought. I mean, it's good for material things, but material things don't make you as happy as you think they will when you're struggling to get by."

He picked up a lamp that needed a new plug, asking, "You have a large family, Miss Rita?"

Emotions in check she smiled, "No. It's just my husband and I. Jack used to be such a great guy..." Realizing she used the past tense, she quickly said, "Is. I mean is. He is a great guy. But the money has sort of changed him."

"Money does that, I suppose," Odis nodded, finding a phillip's head screwdriver the right size for the job. "Could just be the novelty, Miss Rita."

Mighty Fine

"I'm not much better," she sighed. "I guess the novelty of it just wore off quicker in my case. I was never a clothes horse but if you could see my closet now, you'd think it was a warehouse for a clothing outlet."

Odis smiled softly, admiring her honesty.

"I'll never wear it either and that's the part that makes me ill. And I miss 'us'. I don't miss the struggling part, but I loved that even then, we were a team. We'd laugh and snuggle and just--" She blushed, realizing she was babbling like a lunatic. "Sorry. I'm sure you don't need to hear me wallowing when I have so much to be grateful for."

"Everyone needs to talk things out, Miss Rita. Which makes me wonder if you've tried that with your husband?"

"Oh, sure but he doesn't really hear me. He takes what I say and twists it till I think maybe he's right. He took off in this new social class like a duck to water. Me? Not so much. Oh, I do love the house but it's more house than we need. It's a good investment I'm told. But now we joined a country club filled with snobby people...I know that's not nice. Maybe they aren't snobby but I can't help but think they find me...too friendly?" She shrugged and rubbed off the last spot with vigor. "And he became best friends with a man that is nothing like the friends we used to have. He's pompous and crass. I don't know how his girlfriend puts up with him." She stood and tossed the rag in a bucket. "That's better!"

Odis grinned, knowing she was talking about the trunk, but hoping she felt better as well for having a chance to talk things

Linda Voelker

out, "Looks like it's fresh from the department store, Miss Rita."

She laughed. "I wouldn't go that far, Odis, but thanks. And thanks for listening."

"I don't know your husband, but I'm willing to bet he hasn't really changed. Miss Rita, you just keep smiling and love him like you always have. He'll fall right into step with that. You'll see."

"You're such a wonderful man," she replied, moving in and startled him with a hug. "Meeting you has made my whole day." As she stepped back, she noticed the clock on the wall and gasped. "Oh, it's later than I thought. I need to go before Jack gets home from his golf outing. Thank you, Odis," she said sincerely. "I can't tell you what today has done for me, but I'm grateful."

He waited till she grabbed her purse, then walked her to her car. "I'm mighty grateful too, Miss Rita and I know that Miss Thelma is too."

She was pleased to see her car was untouched and got in behind the wheel. "I'll be back. I even know how to use my GPS thingy, thanks to you."

He chuckled and gave her hood a pat. "You drive safe now, and God bless."

"I will. God bless you too, Odis. See you soon!"

Rita had less trouble finding her way home, getting there in time to start dinner before Jack arrived. She decided that what Odis said was exactly what she needed to do. Her being miserable would only drive them apart. Just because their circumstances

Mighty Fine

had changed, nobody said she had to act all hoity toity. And Jack always said that if she was happy, he was happy. It was time to see if that still held true.

Jack came in the door, half dreading being home. He felt guilty over how much he enjoyed seeing Connie, even though they did no more than reminisce about times they shared in the past. You can't be with someone that long without having memories together, he told himself, trying to make sense of his need to see her. It was nice to be with her. Easy. It was as if they had never lost touch, in fact, just picking up where they'd left off.

Well, not quite. He was very aware of the changes. He'd planned on seeing her today to tell her he wouldn't be meeting again, but when Connie mentioned seeing him again, he went along.

He felt that guilt weigh even heavier as he heard Rita singing with the oldies in the kitchen.

"Hey..." He smiled as she jumped a mile, blushing to the roots of her hair. "Sorry...I thought you heard me come in."

"No, I was jammin'," she giggled. "Have a good game?"

"Nah...but it kept me off the streets," he teased, trying to appear normal. "You must have had a good day."

"Oh, I did!" She bit back further explanation and said, "We're having burgers and salad. Is that okay?"

He'd had pizza with Connie, but smiled. "Sounds great." He popped a slice of carrot in his mouth and asked, "So what did you do today?"

She wasn't good at fibbing and knew if he saw her eyes, he'd know. Sticking as close to the truth as she could, she said, "I found a new shop and I met the most precious little boy. His name was Marcus."

Jack plated the burgers as she picked up the salad bowl, "There's a good, strong name."

"There was this trunk and he came up and wondered if it had toys in it," she continued, thanking him when he held her chair. "So I pretended I couldn't get it open and he helped. Oh, Jack, he was so disappointed to find it empty."

He chuckled, imagining the scene she described perfectly. Rita would have been such a great mom. He really did wish things had been different for her on that score.

She passed him the salad dressing. "So, tell me about your day. Did George win?"

"No, a guy named John did," he answered without pause, for he had played nine holes with the guys before meeting with Connie. "He's with the same investment company. Now you'd like him. He reminds me of Dave in a lot of ways."

"Is he married?"

Ignoring the irony, he teased, "In case you've forgotten, woman, you are."

She giggled, swatting his arm, "I was just curious. Maybe we can have them over for dinner some time."

He was surprised she'd even suggest another dinner after the other night, but nodded, "Why not?"

Mighty Fine

"Jack?"

Here we go, he thought, looking at her after taking note of the more serious tone, "Hmm?"

"I want you to know that I love you. We've had so many changes lately, but that's one thing that will never change." She blushed a bit and looked back at her plate. "I just wanted you to know that."

Her words stirred something deep within and he found himself reaching over to tip her chin up, "How hungry are you?"

She frowned and whispered, "What do you mean?"

"Can you hold off on dinner a bit?"

Understanding dawned and she felt that blush sweep over her body. "Uh huh."

"Good." With that, he stood and gathered her up to toss her over his shoulder.

"Jaaaaaaaaack," she squealed, giggling as her heart slammed and she clung to his back.

"Rita," he countered, somehow managing to climb the stairs, knowing he owed it to the gym.

"You're going to break your back," she worried. "Don't you DROP me, Jack!"

He chuckled at her umbrage, dropping her onto their bed with a sexy grin Rita had all but forgotten. As he tugged at her sweater and flung it aside, he nuzzled her neck, "Rita?" When she peeked up, he kissed her softly. "I love you, too," he whispered, never more sure of anything.

Linda Voelker

He then set about proving it.

6

Rita fell into a routine of helping out at the Grace Shop nearly every day for the next two weeks. She felt better than she had in years, even before the win. She owed much of that to Odis. Every day she left him, she felt wiser and touched by his genuine need to help others. It was the second week there that Thelma returned, making a beeline to where Rita was sorting a garbage bag of socks.

"Miss Rita..."

She smiled and hugged her, something Odis was finally getting used to. "Hi, Thelma. Where's the little ones?"

"With my mother. I just wanted to thank you...I know it was you that put that money in the book."

Rita saw what looked like worry on her face and smiled, taking her hand. "I thank you for letting me offer it, Thelma. It was such a gift to know that I could be of help."

Thelma blinked, holding back tears, unsure what to say to that.

"You are such a wonderful mother," Rita continued. "You can see it in your children." She raised her brows, remembering something. "Hey, I think Odis has a pair of shoes if you still need them."

"No, I mean, thank you anyway, but Marcus has a brand new

pair now. And little Reatha has no worries either, Miss Rita."

Rita grinned, glad of that. "I hope you don't mind that Odis shared that your husband was out of work. Has he found a new job yet?"

"No, but he has an interview with the city today. I have everything but my eyes crossed."

Rita laughed, "I am sure he'll find work. I've been praying he does."

Thelma relaxed visibly, "Thank you, Miss Rita. That's nice to know."

Odis came in carrying an old chest of drawers, the knobs missing. He set it down and put his hands on the small of his back, arching a bit.

"Did you ever think to ask one of those teens out there to help," Rita half scolded.

He chuckled, "Don't she sound like my Alva, Miss Thelma?"

Thelma laughed, "She sure does."

"Well, common sense is rather important, Mister Walker," Rita smirked.

He laughed again, moving to get the rest of the things dropped off. Thelma and Rita grinned at one another hearing him call out, "Hey, Rufus, can you give me a hand with this?"

"Quick learner," Thelma giggled.

"No, he's just afraid of me," Rita winked before their laughter filled the shop.

Mighty Fine

Later that day, as Odis and Rita sorted through a few garbage bags filled with clothes, she gave him a nudge with her elbow. "So tell me about you, Odis. I feel you know too much about me," she grinned. "I need to balance things a bit."

He chuckled and said, "I'm not near as interesting, Miss Rita. I grew up not far from here. My momma raised us to be good, God fearin' children. There was me and Rodney and my sister, Odessa."

Rita smiled, folding the clothes, "And your father?"

"Never met him," Odis said, "He died in prison not long after I was born. I'm the baby," he grinned, knowing she'd have to wrap her head around his size and that statement.

"Oh, I'm so sorry about your dad, Odis."

"No need. Momma was enough of a parent to cover both," he remembered with a grin. "She saw to it that we always had food on the table. She worked two steady jobs and took in sewing when she could."

"When did she ever sleep?"

Odis chuckled, "Rarely. Even then I think she kept one eye open. She was a little bitty thing, just under five feet. But let me tell you, if she caught us on the wrong side of right, she was a force to be reckoned with," he grinned.

"Odis," Rita teased, "are you telling me you have done wrong?"

"Oh, many times and in many ways, Miss Rita. But after Momma set me straight and reminded me of all the good she saw

Linda Voelker

in me, I found I didn't like disappointing her so I did try."

"She sounds like a wonderful mother, Odis."

"The best, Miss Rita. The very best." He moved a stack of clothes to start another, holding a faded sweatshirt with Rudolph on it. "We never believed in Santa Claus or the Easter Bunny." He caught the flicker of sadness in Rita's eyes and smiled. "We celebrated the holidays but only for the reason they were meant to be celebrated. Momma knew that if we believed in Santa Claus and had no tree, let alone gifts to go under it, we'd think we weren't good enough. There wasn't a day in my life that I believed that."

Rita smiled, though she had a lump in her throat.

"There was one Christmas though," Odis recalled, a twinkle in his eyes, "that we had us a tree."

"You did?" Rita was glad to hear it. She couldn't imagine never having one.

"Momma had gotten sick. So sick that she couldn't even get out of bed. Had us all scared that we was gonna lose her. When Sunday came she sent us off to church...and when Pastor Sam saw us there without our momma, he knew something was wrong. We told him she was sick...real bad. He came home with us after the service and that night, four full meals came from the church ladies. Momma didn't have to worry about us eatin' that was for sure."

Rita smiled, "Oh...that was so nice."

"Indeed it was, Miss Rita. The next day was Christmas Eve...and Momma was still in bed, but had Rodney and Odessa

Mighty Fine

read the story of the first Christmas from the Bible, just as she had each year before. Then we went to bed." Finished with the clothing he smiled. "How about a cup of coffee, Miss Rita?"

"Sounds good, Odis...thanks." She followed him to the back and asked, "What happened next?"

Pouring two mugs and setting the pot back on the maker, he grinned. "We woke up." Handing her a mug he added, "And for the longest time we thought Momma was proven wrong for once. Santa surely existed and stopped at our place."

Rita grinned back, delighted by his expression and tone.

"There was a tree that had more lights than we could count, right there on our old front porch. And underneath were the prettiest boxes, just waiting for us. It was somethin', Miss Rita. I can tell you that. And Momma got up out of bed when we all scrambled to tell her and I think it was the only time I remember her shedding tears. While we made two trips to cart them all inside to open, she opened an envelope that had her name on it. Inside there were two crisp tens and one five dollar bill." He looked lost in the memory, his eyes twinkling. "I'm here to tell you, Miss Rita, that twenty-five dollars might not seem like much today, but for us, it was like a miracle. Odessa got a new baby doll with its own pink plastic cradle. I can still see her playing with it in the corner of the living room. She'd like to carry that doll with her everywhere. Named her Holly..." He remembered in a surprised tone that he still could. "And Rodney got a football. He went on to get a football scholarship to attend college and I think that seed was planted that day."

Linda Voelker

"And you, Odis?" Rita swallowed hard, though her smile never faltered. "What did you get?"

"Bein' the baby, I got most of my needs met from the things Rodney outgrew....till I outgrew him, that is," he chuckled. "That year I got my very first pair of new shoes. A perfect fit." He shook his head as he grinned. "That was a mighty fine, Christmas, Miss Rita. Mighty fine indeed."

Rita hugged him unexpectedly, giving him barely enough time to hold his mug up out of the way. He chuckled as she pulled back and said, "Sorry, I forgot you were holding coffee."

Eyes twinkling he gave a nod. "My Alva liked to hug as well. I see her as the welcoming angel on the inside of the pearly gates."

"Oh, Odis," Rita whispered, struck by the life this wonderful man had endured.

"No need to be sad, Miss Rita. I know I'll be with her again one day. By the time the cancer took true hold, God answered my prayers and took her home."

"I complain," she managed in a soft, choked whisper, "about things that are so insignificant while having won so much money. How could you stand to be around me?"

He looked at her in a way that left no doubt. "You have heart, Miss Rita. A heart that shines through to everyone that comes in to Grace Shop. Stand you?" He scoffed, his smile back in full force. "It's a mighty fine thing that I have you as a friend."

Rita squeezed him again, then echoed his feelings. "You have no idea how much your friendship means to me, Odis. No

Mighty Fine

idea at all."

It was a few days later that the bell announced another customer. Odis had gone to the hardware store to pick up knobs for the dresser he'd refinished, leaving Rita on her own. Something she had to practically beg him to do, promising him she'd be fine.

She saw a petite blonde woman inching her way in, looking uneasy. Rita quickly greeted her, remembering that feeling well, "Hi there. Can I help you?"

"Oh, yes," she said, obviously surprised to find a white woman. "I'm Mildred and our church had a white elephant and we remembered seeing an article about this charity. The things that didn't sell are on the back of my son's pickup truck. I was wondering if you would be interested in any of it."

Wishing Odis were there, she said, "Oh, how thoughtful. I'm sure Odis would be grateful for anything you have. He ran to the hardware store. Wait, let me see if I can find anyone to help unload the truck."

"Oh, it's okay. My son and his friend are with me. They can unload if you just show them where to put it."

And that's why, when Odis returned, there was no path to get through, and he could hear Rita, but not see her.

"We had a delivery," she called out in a rather muffled voice.

"So I see," he chuckled.

"I didn't know where to have them put it," she explained needlessly.

"Yup, see that too," he grinned, wondering why she didn't think to move to the front before they parked all of the things blocking her in.

"Ah, remember that common sense thing I mentioned the other day?"

"Uh huh, I sure do, Miss Rita," he replied, his words tinged with amusement.

"Well, let's not bring that up, okay?"

He was still chuckling twenty minutes later when he'd finally moved things out of the way to free her.

She smiled sheepishly as she looked up at him. "Oh, and Odis?"

"Yes?"

"There's no need to go spreading tales to Miss Thelma either."

He laughed as she picked up her car keys, following her to her car. "You go home and rest, Miss Rita. You've put in quite a day."

"You're telling me," she countered, getting into the car to sigh. "Thanks again, my friend," she smiled. "See you tomorrow."

"Drive..."

Safely," she finished with a grin. "I will. Bye now," she sang, pulling up the drive and out of the lot to head home.

Jack had decided that seeing Connie, no matter how innocently he wanted to color it, was wrong. While they hadn't done more

Mighty Fine

than hug hello and goodbye, the last time they'd met in a fast food parking lot, things progressed to an unexpected kiss. A kiss both familiar and foreign. But that same kiss was enough to make him realize he was kissing the wrong woman. She didn't seem too surprised when he quickly withdrew, saying he had a meeting he'd forgotten about at the bank. She wasn't a stupid woman though. Connie knew something was changing.

She got out of his truck and blew a kiss, her willingness to pretend she hadn't noticed the change clear. He pulled out of the lot and exhaled, knowing he'd meet her the next day and put an end to everything. Connie represented his past. But Rita held his heart. She was the reason he looked forward to the future and it was high time he proved it.

Some days that start out bad, seem to just stay that way. Jack was there when she got home, talking to the mailman. She beeped seeing them, parked and got out of the car all smiles.

"Hi there!"

Jack grinned. "Hi yourself." He nodded toward the mailman and said, "Clark is retiring. This is his last delivery."

Rita hugged him and said, "You enjoy it. You've earned it. All that walking would do me in."

He grinned, "Thanks. Me and the missus are going to head down to Florida. Seems that's what all the old folks do now."

"You're not old," Rita said. "You're the new middle age because I'll be the new twenty soon."

Jack laughed and hugged her to his side, and they both waved goodbye to Clark. Rita started to the house and Jack said, "Aren't you forgetting something?"

"What?"

"Pop the trunk, lady. I'll carry in your bags."

She froze. "I..I ah, don't have any."

"You weren't shopping?"

Had the conversation gone any other way, she wouldn't have panicked. But she wasn't one to out and out lie. "No, I was, ah...doing charity work."

Jack wasn't surprised that she'd be so inclined, but was surprised she hadn't mentioned it. She went inside before he could ask about it and he suddenly realized she was hiding something.

He found her heading up the stairs and said, "Rita, come here a minute."

"I'll be back down in a minute, Hon. I just want to shower." And think!

"It can wait. Come here, babe."

Feeling more trapped than she had in the Grace Shop, she came back down the stairs.

"Why haven't I heard about your charity work before now?"

She shrugged and said, "It's just never come up, that's all. But I really do love it, Jack. It makes me feel so good to be part of something so meaningful."

He moved to the sofa and patted the spot beside him when

Mighty Fine

he sat. She reluctantly joined him.

"So tell me about it. What's the charity?" He put his arm around her shoulder and gave her a soft squeeze. "Is that what you've been doing these last few weeks? I'd wondered about the change in you."

She looked at him, her eyes pleading. "Yes, and I'm sorry I didn't mention it, I just didn't want you to tell me I couldn't..."

"Rita," he frowned, "Why would you think such a thing?"

"B-Because it's on the west end of town in a church basement." There. She said it.

His arm moved from her as he shifted on the couch to look at her in disbelief, "You've been driving to the west end on your own for two weeks?"

She stiffened, knowing he was going to be upset. "And I'm fine...nothing happened. And Odis walks me to my car and it's right behind the church and nobody even bothers it. They know me from the shop..."

He came to his feet, his eyes flashing, "Are you out of your mind, Rita?!"

She jumped up as well, ready for the battle even if she wouldn't win the war. "No! I love that shop and I love everyone that comes in. Do you remember my telling you about Marcus, the little boy? I met him there and his mom, Thelma. They're such good people and they're so grateful for everything they find that they can use. Her husband is out of work and they don't have any other way to get clothing or shoes...or things for the baby."

Knowing she was on a roll, Jack held up his hand, "Listen, Honey, I know you have a big heart and I know you like helping out where you can. But there is no way I can let you go back there." He felt sick just thinking she'd been there. "What if something had happened to you, Rita? I didn't even know where you were!"

"But nothing did! Jack, I'm not careless. I'm escorted in and out all the time by Odis..."

"Rita. Enough. I'm sorry, but it's not a place I feel you should be. Just turn on the news or read the paper. I'm not being unreasonable here."

"I did read the paper and that's how I found out about Odis." She glared. "I didn't have to tell you!"

Jack scowled, imagining how things might have unfolded and paced, "I know why you didn't tell me, Rita. And you do too. I wouldn't have allowed you to go. I would have put a stop to it happening in the first place and that's why you didn't tell me. That alone shows you knew you were doing something you shouldn't be doing! There are shootings there all the time."

"I don't do anything but drive there and go inside. I don't walk around the streets," she retorted desperately. "Jack, they're good people. Odis...Thelma...they matter to me, Jack."

"Drive by shooting occur in cars, Rita. They happen on the streets, sidewalks, walking into a church!"

"But that's not their fault! And people are in need there, Jack! I don't think Odis even owns a gun!"

"Odis, whoever that is," Jack snorted. "I...said...no. That's the end of it, Rita."

"B-But they need--"

"We've donated half a million dollars to charities already. We've done our part. I'm done talking about this, Rita and you're done lying to me. It ends now!"

She watched him stride to his study before she flew upstairs to slam the bedroom door. It was there that she cried herself to sleep.

Rita sat staring at the phone, knowing she had to call Odis, but unable to actually do it.

Last night had been horrible. She woke when Jack came up to bed, the silence between them pointed. There was so much she wanted to say, but she knew it wouldn't matter. He wouldn't change his mind.

All night she lay there staring at the ceiling, recalling everything that transpired the last few weeks, her heart breaking at the thought of never going again.

In the morning, Jack spoke after he'd showered and dressed, "I have a meeting today but I will be back by noon. I suggest you call that Odis guy, and tell him to find someone else because your days there are done. Do not test me, Rita."

She hadn't even looked at him, her eyes still on the ceiling. He didn't take time to make coffee before she heard the front door close not five minutes later.

Rita felt the click of the door, resounding somewhere deep

within. It was such a final sound, like the ending of any hope of making things work between them.

Jack was still amazed that Rita would do something so crazy. As he drove down the well maintained streets of what he'd once viewed as mansions, he felt a pang of deep shame for his own craziness. Who was he to find fault with Rita? He was on his way to meet Connie. Rita sure deserved better.

He stopped at the light, willing himself to turn around and go home, but knew he had to see Connie. When the light changed, he drove on, caught in a web of his own making.

Rita gave up rehearsing what she'd say to Odis. It was impossible. In her mind she would get out hello, and Odis would say in that happy baritone voice, "Hello, Miss Rita," and she burst into tears just thinking about it.

She jumped as the phone rang, blinking a moment before taking the call. "Hello?"

"Hi there, sunshine. Long time no see! How's life treating you?"

"Tina?"

"Yes, I'm sorry it took so long to get back to you. My sister was staying with us because Bruce was out of town. She was in the last few months of her pregnancy and absolutely miserable! It's been crazy here. How are you?"

Mighty Fine

Valiant effort was needed to lie so well. "Fine...we're fine." She gripped the phone tighter and casually asked, "How's Dave? How's everyone?" Her voice cracked as she added, "And the people that are in our house? They seemed so nice..." She cleared her throat to softly say, "I've really missed you, Tina."

"Okay, my friend, what's wrong?" Tina knew her well enough to know when she was troubled. "Please don't tell me it's because it took me so long to call you back. I couldn't take the guilt," she teased.

"N-No...I just...it's just..."

When that was all she got, Tina said, "I think it's time we got together, don't you? Want to come over or should I travel to that higher ground?"

Unable to appreciate the joke, Rita sniffled, "I'll come there, if that's okay?"

"Of course. I'll whip up some dip and we'll right the world eating veggies and drinking my make it yourself iced tea. See you in about an hour?"

"Sure...and Tina?"

"Yeah?"

"Thanks."

7

As she drove the familiar streets of the old neighborhood, she realized she hadn't called Odis. Then again, she hadn't left a note for Jack either, saying she'd gone to see Tina. She realized she was relieved about the first, and didn't really care about forgetting the latter.

She stopped at the light and glanced at the park the guys used to play softball in. She smiled, remembering the good times shared there. For all their worries about money, they really were happy. Life here was different. People were different. If one person needed anything, everyone jumped in to help. In the new neighborhood, nobody even bothered with each other. They were beautiful houses, but it seemed that's all they were. You rarely saw the people that lived in them.

The light changed and she drove on, slowing down as she came to their old house. It looked the same, but her flowerbed was gone. Gnomes were in a line along the wall that once had marigolds. The front door was open and she wished she could just pull in the drive and go inside. Of course, the Millers that bought it, wouldn't appreciate her moving back in, but she smiled at the thought of trying. She wondered if Jack would even care. Probably not. His life would run smoother without her in it. He could run with George and revel in being in the big leagues.

Mighty Fine

Tina was at the door as she pulled up, grinning ear to ear as she hurried out to hug her. "Oh...it's so good to see you!"

Prolonging the hug, Rita whispered, "Right back atcha." Pulling back she grinned, her eyes searching Tina's face. "You don't know how good it is to see you."

"Come on, ya nut...before we have the neighbors spreading the rumor I'm cheating on Dave."

Laughing, Rita followed Tina into the house that had once been as familiar to her as her own. Nothing had changed and it felt warm and welcoming.

"I made tea, but have wine. What would you like to start with?"

Settling at the small kitchen table, Rita smiled. "Iced tea is perfect." She picked up a slice of carrot and dunked it in the dip. "So is this," she decided, remembering the dip she could never duplicate no matter how many times she'd tried. "I still say you never shared that one secret ingredient to make this dip, Teen."

Laughing, she poured the iced tea and brought them to the table. "Love you as I do, there's so few things I can do better. Let's just leave it at that," she winked.

"IIIIIIIIIIIIIIII knew it," Rita grinned. "You stinker!"

A few minutes later, having fully depleted their bantering, Tina looked at her pointedly. "So, tell me what's really going on, Rita. I know you too well for you to say nothing, so don't try it."

"I don't know where to start and I know that whatever I say will sound ludicrous. After all I should be grateful." Sighing, her finger running around the rim of her glass, Rita said, "We let the

Linda Voelker

money change us. I'm quick to see the changes in Jack, but I let it change me too."

"Heck, I'd love to have the money to change but that's nothing," Tina scoffed. "Which reminds me, how was Hawaii?"

Smiling softly, Rita said, "Beautiful, it really is. But it would have been even more so if you and Dave were there."

"Damn straight," Tina joked. "I'd still be walking around in my leis, carrying a drink with a chunk of pineapple and a little pink umbrella."

Rita grinned before it wobbled.

"Hey..." Tina reached over to cover her hand. "Is it Jack? Is he running around on you?"

"No, it's not another woman. It's his financial adviser, George. He won't let me be with Odis anymore and that's the only pleasure I had in my life..."

"Wait...slow down." Tina was frowning. "Jack's gay? Who the heck is Odis?!"

Rita let out a watery laugh. "No, Jack's just with him a lot always going over money things. And I really don't like George. He's crass and arrogant and thinks he's better than everyone else."

"Whewwwwwwww," Tina exaggerated her relief. "I mean... Jack was so into you, that I couldn't wrap my head around him being gay!" She took the celery stalk Rita had picked up from her, needing to know, "Who's Odis?"

Rita looked at her friend and sighed, "He runs a shop out of the basement of a church for the needy. I found an article in the

Mighty Fine

paper about him."

"I remember," Tina nodded. "Looks kinda like that guy in the Green Mile."

"Yes! But he sounds like Barry White with his deep voice. I love his voice," Rita added wistfully.

"Connect the dots for me. I don't get the problem." Tina bit into the celery, watching Rita as she chewed it.

"I went to the shop...to donate money. That's all. I just wanted to do something with the money that would help others. Oh, I know we donated to charities...but this was different. And once I went I fell in love with Odis and everyone else there."

Holding up her hand, Tina said, "Define that 'fell in love' part."

Rolling her eyes, "Tinaaaaaaaaaaaa."

"Well, I'm still trying to figure out what's wrong," Tina sighed. "So far Jack is keeping an eye on his money and you're donating it. OH!" She sat straighter. "Is that it?"

"No. Well, I didn't even tell him I did. I just returned a dress I'd never wear and donated that money. It's just that he won't let me go back to the church," Rita frowned. "I know what the news reports say but nothing bad happened to me."

"Sweetie, Dave wouldn't want me there either and he doesn't even like me half the time," she joked. "Jack doesn't want anything to happen to you because he loves you...that's all."

Tsk." Rita scowled at the one that was supposed to be on her side. "If you went once, Tina then you'd understand. The people there are no different than us, but they're so much better in ways.

Linda Voelker

They're so grateful for the things others would toss out, if not for Odis. And Odis is an amazing man, Tina. I really like him."

"Doesn't Jack?"

"He's never met him..."

Tina frowned, "So take him."

Rita sat back and blinked at Tina, "I didn't even give that a thought!"

Tina chuckled and popped the celery into her mouth. "You must be stressed. You always liked bringing people together." Selecting a carrot, she dipped it before pointing at Rita with it. "Remember when the Smiths and Kings were at odds over their property lines? You, Miss Mary Sunshine, had a cookout and kept making comments about how half a foot didn't mean much unless you were stuck mowing it."

Giggling at the memory she said, "Do you remember how ticked Jack was? I thought he was going to kill me for not leaving them to deal with it themselves."

"Uh huh. Did you know they went on vacation together two months ago? Ya did good, my friend."

"This situation isn't as simple," Rita sighed. "But, I think giving Jack a chance to meet them could just do the trick."

Tina uncorked the wine and grabbed two glasses. "Don't get too hopeful, Ree. The shop is still in the wrong end of town."

"I know." She shifted on the chair, that moment of hope waning. "New topic. Think fast."

"Dave's going bald. I'm getting fat though, so I can't kick."

And that's why Rita loved Tina so much. She was a quick

Mighty Fine

thinker.

Jack was waiting for Connie when she pulled into the park, her smile bright. He managed a smile, knowing how difficult the next few minutes would be.

"How are you, handsome? Were you waiting long?"

He was sitting on the picnic table, and didn't rise hoping to avoid a hug. "No. Just got here a few minutes ago. We need to talk, Connie."

He watched her smile fade, her expression shifting to one of dread. "About?"

"I just can't do this anymore, Connie. I'm sorry."

Without missing a beat, she hissed, "Oh, so once again, you get to decide when to call it quits. Do you have any idea how deeply you hurt me when you left me to marry someone else? We were together for years, Jack. I loved you. And damn it, you said you loved me! Why, Jack? What does she have that I don't have? That's what I need to know. I saw her, she's dumpy, if you ask me. And Jack, I'm not vain, but I know I'm prettier," she choked out, struggling not to cry.

"Connie," he soothed, "Don't do this. If you think I set out to hurt you, you're wrong. I didn't expect to feel the way I did for Rita...and I can't tell you what made me fall in love so quickly. I just knew that I couldn't imagine my life without her in it."

Connie stiffened, her eyes flashing. "So why did you call me back? Did you just need to see if you could still keep me dangling on your string? Was I some game to you?!"

"No." He sighed and looked at her, "I don't know. Seeing you brought back good memories of our time together, Connie. I don't even understand why I wanted to see you again, but I did. The thing is, Con, I love my wife. She's beautiful from the inside out and I just don't want to risk losing her."

Connie turned away for a moment, stiff and struggling to regain her emotions. She'd known she was meeting with Jack for her own reasons, and none of them had to do with love. She was simply out to prove something.

Jack held his breath as he watched her during her moment of reflection. In that moment he realized Connie had the power to end his marriage. She could track Rita down and tell her they'd been seeing one another, their meeting times alone more than enough proof. The thought actually terrified him.

What seemed an eternity later, but was only a moment or two, Connie turned and looked at him, much calmer. "Jack. I'm happy for you. Really. And maybe I needed this, to see you and have a chance to get things off my chest." She offered a wobbly smile. "Go home to your wife, Jack. Be happy."
Jack exhaled, coming to his feet. He hugged her tight, whispering, "You too, Connie. Maybe someday you and Emerson can come over for dinner."

Her laugh was broken, but she said, "He is a good guy. Maybe now I'll give him more of a chance."

Jack smiled, hoping so. "Take care, Connie."

"Bye, Jack."

Mighty Fine

He drove home feeling as if the weight of the world had lifted from his shoulders. He just wanted to go home and find Rita. He wanted to hold her close and make things right between them once more.

Not only did he go home to find the house empty, there was no note to explain where she was. He couldn't believe she'd go back to the shop after their talk last night, but she wasn't going to be there long.

He went back out to his truck and drove to the church, planning to get Rita out of there. The drive itself only made things worse. His jaw was clenched so tightly it hurt by the time he pulled into the lot of the church. Slamming the door when he parked, he went inside the basement, barely noticing the bell that announced his arrival. He stood just inside the door, scanning the clutter to find his wife.

"Hello there, Sir. What can I do for you today?"

Jack looked at the man that spoke and realized he had to be Odis. He looked like a quarterback. A tall one. "I'm looking for my wife, Rita. Is she here?"

Odis lost his smile as his concern became clear. "No, sir, I haven't seen her today. I had no way of checking on her though. I hope she's okay."

Jack swore as he pulled out his cell phone, punching her cell number and waiting. He had visions of her being carjacked and laying dead somewhere.

After the fourth ring, he heard, "Hi, Jack..." He exhaled, then heard her giggle. "You'll never guess where I am..."

He felt his anger surface once more, his relief at hearing her voice overpowered by it. "I don't care where you are, Rita. Get home...Now!"

Odis watched as he ended the call and turned to leave.

"Mr. Jack?"

Jack paused, his hand on the doorknob.

"I just wanted to tell you how fortunate you are to have a woman like Miss Rita to call your own."

Jack slowly exhaled, remembering that he told Connie the same thing. Knowing how much Rita looked up to the man, he let go of the doorknob and faced him fully. "I appreciate that. I also appreciate you watching out for her."

His cell rang and he took it from his pocket and took a deep breath seeing it was Rita. In a softer tone he asked, "So where are you?"

Rita, who had jumped up from the table when he was so furious, frowned, the fight in her confused. "At Tina's and I neither liked or deserved the tone you used before, buster."

He heard Tina's voice sing out, "Hellooooooooo, Jack!"

"When do you plan to be home," he asked, not wanting their private issues to become so public.

"I don't know," she mused, dripping with sarcasm "When do you want me home, Daddy?"

He snorted, counting to three out of ten before managing, "I'll leave it up to you. Tell Tina I said hi." And with that, he once again pocketed the phone.

A little boy had joined Odis during Jack's moment of exasperation, coming up to the man's kneecaps. Odis rubbed the boys head and asked, "Marcus...would you like to say hello to Miss Rita's husband? His name is Mr. Jack."

Marcus moved to hide behind Odis when he realized Jack was looking at him, his head peeking out to study him with one chocolate brown eye. Jack had to smile. He was a cute kid. "I hear you and Rita...ah, Miss Rita...found an old treasure chest?"

"Oder there," Marcus felt the need to point out, one index finger indicating the location.

"You in a hurry, Mr. Jack?" Odis smiled in a way that relaxed Jack, and that was saying something. "I put on a pot of coffee, and Miss Thelma, Marcus' Momma, brought in some banana bread she baked this morning."

Considering the last place Jack wanted to be was there, he shocked himself by saying, "Sounds good."

He couldn't help but notice the walls needed patching and a good coat of paint. Thelma joined them as they reached the back.

"Marcus, what did I tell you about leaving my side?" Odis smiled at her. "I was introducin' Marcus to Mr. Jack..."

"You're Miss Rita's husband? Is she here? I was wondering why she was late today," the woman smiled.

"No, she's not here. She's visiting an old friend of ours." He wasn't used to all the Miss and Mister stuff, but chalked it up to manners. "I guess she didn't call you today?"

Odis handed him a cup of coffee as Thelma placed banana

bread on a napkin for him with ease, considering the baby balanced on her hip. "No, sir. But I don't believe she's ever phoned. Miss Rita pops up like the sunshine after a rain. Makes me happy every time I see her."

Jack wasn't surprised she failed to make the call he'd demanded of her, but his jaw clenched anyway before he said, "I don't want her on this side of town."

It seemed as if his words hung there a moment, echoing, before Thelma finally said, "Which means...."

"Which means he loves Miss Rita and is concerned. Rightly so," Odis provided. "Can't say I wasn't worried myself, Mr. Jack. She's got a good heart and fails to see folks can have anything less."

Jack appreciated his understanding. "It's nothing personal. She speaks very highly of you..." He looked at Thelma and her family then, to add, "...all."

Thelma stood a bit straighter, the chubby baby on her hip holding the neck of her shirt. "She's been a good friend to all of us. I owe her a lot. If not for that money--" She stopped when Jack frowned, realizing he must not have known. She reached for Marcus' hand and said, "Please tell her I'll miss her. Come on, Marcus. It's time we went home."

Odis didn't miss Jack's reaction either. When Thelma left, he said in that soft roll of thunder way, "Marriage is a mighty fine thing, Mr. Jack. As much as I loved my Alva, I still remember the work it took to get it right."

Jack shot him a look. "Pardon?" If the guy thought for

Mighty Fine

one minute, he was going to listen to some lecture, he'd set him straight. Everything about that one word, proved it.

"My Alva was a little, bitty slip of a thing. I might have fit her in my pocket," he smiled, "and often wished I could. But tiny as she was, she was headstrong. She wouldn't abide by my wishes like some genie in a bottle, that's for sure," he chuckled. "Did you ever see one of those little dogs that don't seem to know what a big dog could do to it? That's how Alva was with me." He leaned on the counter and chuckled again. "Truth is, I was afraid of her half the time."

"I don't mean to sound rude," Jack cut in, not up for story time, "but I need to get home." He and Rita were going to have a long talk. That she'd obviously donated money after that half a million had really ticked him off. Even more than that though, rather ironically, it was that she'd kept it from him.

"I understand, Mr. Jack. Once Alva took her wedding band to the hawk shop," he continued, eyes still twinkling. "We didn't have two pennies to rub together and I was working them days in a brick yard. You'd have thought after ten hour days working with brick, I'd know better how to handle that hard headed woman." He stood straight and chuckled again. "I didn't stand a chance." He clapped Jack's shoulder and said, "You be careful going home now, Mr. Jack. It was a pleasure meeting you."

Telling himself he couldn't just walk out mid-story, Jack found himself saying, "I guess I have a few more minutes." He lifted the coffee cup to his mouth so he wouldn't say more, ticked off at himself for wanting to hear the rest.

Linda Voelker

"Good, good," Odis beamed. "Alva helped out a family from the outskirts of the community, over on the hill. They hit some hard times and Alva would clean and cook, tending to the Missus while she was sick. We all was strugglin' a bit more in those days. Alva and I rotated and juggled bills to get by." Jack sure remembered those days.

"Anyway, the Henderson's had two girls and a boy as I recall. The middle child was a boy, Percy they called him. Alva had a soft spot for him, said he was sort of odd child out. Never knew what she meant by that, but with Alva, unless you had a few hours to find out, ya just didn't ask." He chuckled and shook his head. "Could be why I'm that way now. Didn't have much use for a voice box back then," he winked.

Jack smiled, then finished the banana bread, drawn into the tale.

"One day, it was a Sunday in church, I reached for her hand. Oh, ya know how we men do that sometimes, even in church," he mused with fond memory. "I can still feel her skin under this thumb," he said, holding up his right one that looked like half an Italian sausage. "Skin so soft on top, for how hard those hands worked. Anyway, there was no sign of the ring. I lifted it and then frowned at her. She tugged it free of my hand and covered it with her other hand, her eyes on Preacher Sam. He was a young whippersnapper in them days. Well, let me tell you, Mr. Jack, that was the longest preachin' service I ever did sit through. I just wanted to ask her where her wedding band was. Took me half a year to save up for that ninety eight dollar sign of my love."

Mighty Fine

Jack thought of Rita's rings and gave a nod. Crystal thought they screamed cheap.

"We shook hands with Pastor Sam and before we even hit the street, I asked about the ring. She stood up straight, her eyes flashing. 'Odis Walker--'" He chuckled and said, "When she used my last name it always took me back to my momma when she was vexed. They both did that. Her finger was pointed skyward, she only came up to here," he grinned, using his hand to mark off a spot not all that far from his navel. "So she says, 'Odis Walker, were you listening to the sermon at all? I had something material and the Henderson's had need. And if you think I need a ring around my finger to prove you love me, then you best get busy praying!"

He laughed, and Jack found himself grinning too. "She stormed off down the sidewalk like a wet, black hen...clipped, bristly like. And the strangest thing happened, Mr. Jack. That shame I was so sure she'd feel, was mine. Darndest thing. And I did do me some praying. Found myself thanking the Man Upstairs for blessing me with such a hardheaded, loving wife." He paused, his smile dimming a bit, but still clear. "I miss her bad, Mr. Jack. But one day I'll be with her again. It's not God I worry about answerin' to, it's my Alva."

Suddenly, Jack understood why Rita was so upset about not seeing Odis again. Just as suddenly, he lost his anger with her as well. Thanking God he came to he senses about Connie, he set the cup down and held out his hand. Big as his own hands were, they were nothing compared to the one that held it. "Thanks,

Linda Voelker

Odis. Maybe I'll bring Rita down again when we can both spend some time."

Beaming once again, Odis nodded. "I'd like that, Mr. Jack."

Driving home, which an hour ago would have been spent planning his argument with Rita, was spent in reflection from his visit with Odis. If things were different, he knew they'd be friends. The thought brought him up short. He could almost hear Rita and Alva scold, "Why do things have to be different?"

By the time he parked, he still couldn't come up with the right answer.

8

Rita was flipping the channels on the TV, her face in a scowl. She'd come home only to find Jack wasn't there and that infuriated her. If this was his way of paying her back for not leaving a note, she was too frustrated to learn a thing. Other than how she couldn't wait to see him to tell him off.

The door opened and she dropped the remote on the couch to stand, hands on her hips, "Where were you, Jack!?"

He tossed his keys on the table in the foyer, silently drinking her in. She stood straighter, eyes narrowing even more when he smiled.

"OH...I'm so glad you're amused," she all but sneered.

"You can be such an--"

"I was at the church."

Her hands fell from her hips as she blinked, "What did you say?"

He walked in to join her, sitting on the couch to tug her down beside him. "I thought you were there, so I went to the church."

She'd gone from fury to amazed disbelief. "Y-You met Odis?"

He nodded, not allowing his expression to change, "And a few others. Thelma seemed pretty touched by the money you gave her."

Rita shifted, thoughts trying to catch up, but knowing he

wouldn't be happy about the money. "I just took back a dress that I didn't need...It wasn't--"

He placed a finger over her lips, looking her in the eye, "Rita. The issue isn't the money. We used to trust one another. I never once feared you were doing anything behind my back." Thinking of his own guilt he added, "You always knew where I was as well."

Her eyes lowered, knowing as much as she hated to admit it, he was right.

Tipping her chin, he saw her eyes puddling with tears. "I never had to worry about your safety. I trusted you to be where you were supposed to be."

"B-But--"

"Shh, let me finish. When I got home earlier to find you gone, I knew you'd gone to the church again and I was pissed. All the way there, I felt that sick knot in my stomach, like I used to feel when money was tight and I didn't know how the hell we were going to make it till our next pay."

Rita blinked, her vision clearing as tears escaped at last. She knew that feeling. She was feeling it now as well. He was going to tell her he wanted a divorce.

"The win, Rita, stopped that worry. We could breathe, live... do anything we wanted to do." His thumbs worked to wipe her tears. "I knew without a doubt, we'd be happy. We'd always been happy together...so to think money wouldn't add to that was ridiculous."

She whimpered, "Please...Please, Jack..."

Mighty Fine

"Shhhh." He stood, knowing if he sat there, he'd never get out what had to be said. He walked to the fireplace and stopped to face her again. "But we aren't happy. Not the way we used to be. Everything is a battle and I'm not saying it's you. I'm saying we just see the money differently. I see it as a wonderful thing, while you see it as something bad."

She stood, knowing she was going to be sick. "I don't want a divorce, please."

"Divorce," he frowned, his shock clear. "I don't want to divorce either," he quickly said. "I want us to find what we had. I want to be the man you once respected. I haven't been, Ree. I want us to be happy again."

She flew to him, his arms around her instantly to hold her close as she cried. "We can, Jack, we just have to forget we won that money, right?"

He made an amused sound, but knew what she meant. "We don't have to make it our focus, baby, that's all. It's not a bad thing to have won and I think that's still part of the problem. I think you feel almost guilty, Ree, but it's a good thing, not a bad."

"I don't know. I just love you and miss us."

"We're here, Ree together." He kissed her softly and whispered, "Better days are coming, right?"

Hearing that phrase, she smiled and nodded, cupping his head to kiss him again, "We just have to let them."

Over a dinner that Jack made, omelets and toast, they caught up on their day. Odis, of course, was the first topic of conversation, "Isn't he something, Jack? I never met anyone like him."

He smiled, "Me either. He would be impossible to find fault with. And man, is he big."

Giggling, she nodded, "And you met little Marcus? He's the one I told you about that day with the trunk."

"Yeah, he even showed me where it was. 'Oder there'," he chuckled. "His mother, Thea?"

"Thelma," Rita corrected, "She's a great mom."

"Yes, I doubt Marcus or that little sister of his will step out of line too often."

Sipping her coffee, she said, "Being a parent is hard, but I imagine it's much harder to be one on so poor. Her husband had been out of work a long time. They didn't have a way to even meet their bills and that's why I gave her that money from the dress. It was the first day I went. I just tucked it in a book for Marcus. I didn't want to offend her by handing it to her."

Odis came to mind and he was glad for the wisdom he'd shared. Looking at Rita, he was struck again by how beautiful she was. How giving.

"I still don't want you to go back, Rita. You know that, right?"

Ignoring the lump that formed in her throat immediately, she nodded, "I understand," she softly admitted. "I just wish I could."

That night they made love slowly, with a sweet, tender passion that still left them weak and spent. It was a testimony

Mighty Fine

to their new beginning. Old and familiar, but refocusing each of them on how much they loved one another.
    They drifted off to sleep entwined and content once more.

Epilogue

It was two days later that Jack came home to find Rita in the kitchen, putting away groceries. She offered a smile, but her thoughts were never far from missing The Grace Shop. And Jack was gone all day yesterday, making it even harder for Rita to not wallow in her misery. He'd gotten a call from that John he'd met golfing, and helped him cut down trees or something. Turning to put the milk in the fridge, she asked, "Hey, how did it go?"

Jack noted the smile that didn't quite reach her eyes and knew she was grieving for what she felt he was denying her. But he'd been working on a surprise that he knew would change all of that.

"Good," he said, taking her by the hand. "Leave that. We'll get it when we get back."

Confused, she frowned. "Back, from where?"

He ushered her out the door to the truck. "It's a nice day. We're going for a ride."

"But I invited Tina and Dave over tonight, for cards. I have to make dip! I think she gave me the missing ingredient."

"Good. I look forward to seeing them."

She gasped as he lifted her to sit her on the seat, grinning as he winked and closed the door. What had gotten into him, she wondered, watching him round the front of the truck to get in.

Mighty Fine

"You're in a good mood," she smiled, "What's going on?"

He turned on the radio in response, the volume loud enough to hopefully distract her from questioning him.

Rita frowned, studying him, then reached over to touch his hair. "What is that? You have something in your hair, it looks like paint."

He brushed her hand away and scoffed, "Paint? You know I hate to paint." That much was true. Which was why he was so grateful that Odis could gather so many helpers for the work they'd done in the shop.

"Jack, where are you taking me? I didn't even bring my purse. Did we lock the front door?" He turned off the main road and her heart tripped. "Jack..." She knew this route and where it lead, "Are we going to the church? I mean...this is the way..."

Again, no reply, just that smile.

She squirmed, sure of it minutes later, "Jack! You are! You're taking me back to the shop!" She moved to hug him but he wouldn't allow it.

"Behave, woman. I'm driving."

She was so excited she kept fidgeting more the closer they got, babbling, "I can't believe it. I'm so happy, Jack. This is the best surprise evvvvvvvver. Oh, I love you."

She gasped audibly when the church came into view. It was freshly painted, the door a rich red that meant it was fully paid for. She knew Jack had a hand in that and she blinked back tears. A magnitude of colors outlined the building, a vast array of flowers now planted. Overwhelmed, she squeezed his thigh and whispered, "Oh, Jack."

As they pulled into the lot behind the church, Odis stepped outside, his grin ear to ear.

"Well, now," he beamed, "If it's not Miss Rita and Mr. Jack!"

Rita flew to hug him, squeezing as tight as she could, "Odis, I've missed you."

He chuckled, as he said, "I've missed you too, Miss Rita. Everyone has."

Jack joined them and grinned, "You missed your calling, Odis. That would have earned you an Oscar."

Rita frowned, her smile still showing in spite of it. "What do you mean, Jack?"

"He knew we were coming," he replied, pulling out his cell phone to punch in a number. "Okay, Dave, bring 'em on in."

Rita frowned, wondering if Dave was Tina's Dave. Then she saw a big U-Haul pulling in. It was Dave! His hair really was thinning, but he looked great as he drove that truck in, a huge grin on his face. Another U-haul was behind it with Tina behind the wheel and she was laughing.

"Jack," Rita managed, already emotional to begin with.

When Dave jumped out of the truck and went to the back to open the door, Rita covered her mouth and trembled. It was filled to the top with furniture and appliances.

Tina hopped out of the second truck and said, "I need help with the damn door, oh, excuse me. That damn slipped," she frowned, sighing to add, "Twice now."

Rita laughed and cried as Jack unlatched the door to reveal

Mighty Fine

boxes upon boxes of toys, clothes, bedding and canned goods all brand new for the shop.

A parade of people, led by Thelma and her family, were soon there too, hugging Rita and Jack, thanking them for what they'd done. Rita couldn't have spoken if her life depended on it. Sobbing did that to her.

"You were right, baby," Jack said, pulling her close. "I did let the money change me. In ways I refused to see." He thought of Connie and how close he'd come to crossing the line even further, so grateful he'd come to his senses in time.

"Jack, I love you so much."

He kissed her and whispered, "You know I love you too, Ree. I haven't shown it lately, but God, I love you." He kissed her quickly then added, "I let George go too. I went with John. You should have seen his face, but I'll tell you about that later. We need to unload this stuff."

She clung to him, her eyes shimmering with love. "I have never been so proud to be your wife."

The unloading could wait Jack decided, cupping the back of her head to give her a kiss that curled her toes.

Odis drank in the sight of the community unloading the trucks, careful not to disturb the couple that had just given them all a reason to celebrate.

"Love sure is a mighty fine thing," he beamed, "A mighty fine thing indeed."

He knew Alva agreed. He knew it with all his heart.